Caffeine Nigl

D0247706

Abide with Me

Ian Ayris

Fiction aimed at the heart
and the head...

Published by Caffeine Nights Publishing 2012

Copyright © Ian Ayris 2012

Ian Ayris has asserted his right under the Copyright, Designs and Patents Act 1998 to be identified as the author of this work

Published in Great Britain by Caffeine Nights Publishing

www.caffeine-nights.com

British Library Cataloguing in Publication Data.
A CIP catalogue record for this book is available from the British Library

ISBN: 978-1-907565-12-0

Cover design by
Mark (Wills) Williams

Everything else by
Default, Luck and Accident

Ian Ayris

Ian Ayris was born in Dagenham, Essex, in August 1969. Having spent most of his childhood more interested in kicking a tennis ball about the school playground with his mates than actually learning anything, he managed to leave the public education system in 1985 with but two O' Levels and a handful of C.S.E.'s,

And a love of writing.

His academic achievements set him up nicely for the succession of low paid jobs he has maintained to this day. These jobs have included a three year stint as a delivery boy for an electrical company, five years putting nuts and bolts in boxes in a door factory, one day in a gin factory, and three months in a record shop, He has spent the last sixteen years, however, working with adults with learning difficulties, and in the meantime, has become a qualified counsellor.

Ian's love of writing resurfaced late in his thirties, in the guise of short stories. He has since had almost thirty short stories published both in print and online, and is currently studying for a degree in English Literature.

Ian lives with his wife and three children in Romford, Essex, and is a lifelong Dagenham and Redbridge supporter.

ACKNOWLEDGEMENTS

Firstly, I'd like to thank my friends from the early days over at FS – special mentions to Brooke, Jude, Macka, Ray, Sarah Beth, and Jo Lynn. Thank you all – for everything. Couldn't have made it without you. And over at Ch79 – Ragna, Janie, Gav, and Claire. Thanks, guys. Your words, wise and kind, pushed me right to the end.

To Elodie and Sue for beta reading the early drafts. Your support and encouragement will stay in my heart for a very long time. Thank you.

And thanks also to everyone at Caffeine Nights for their continued support throughout the publishing of this book. Special mentions to Carol and Bob, Alison, Jools, and Darren. And Mr Nick Quantrill, a brilliant writer and a great friend. Cheers, mate.

Thanks also to Graeme Howlett and his fantastic West Ham website – Knees Up Mother Brown (http://kumb.com/) And thanks also to all the other diehard Hammers out there who helped me with some of the football details in the book. Especially my best mate, Tony – a scholar and a gentleman. A Hammer through and through.

If I've left anyone out, please forgive me. The writing of this book really does feel like one big group effort Thank you all.

Finally, thank you to my parents for the constant belief and encouragement they gave me throughout the writing of this book.

And my sister, Louise, for showing me what courage is.

Real Reviews from Real Readers

'Ian Ayris' debut novel combines grit, pathos and humour in a skilful mix that's rarer than a Trevor Brooking diving header.'
Howard Linskey - 'Best-selling author of 'THE DROP'

'An unforgettable first outing into the world of fiction.'
Graeme Howlett - editor. Knees Up Mother Brown (KUMB)

'I suspect nothing I say will do it justice, so I'll say, read it, now. And leave it at that.'
Josh Stallings - Author of Beautiful, Naked, and Dead

'I read it in just two sittings, and was thoroughly engaged throughout.'
Paul Hatt - Football Book Reviews

'An astonishing depiction of a harsh life and social dysfunction in the London East End'
Professor Brian Stoddart - Former Vice-Chancellor and President at La Trobe University, Australia

'Ayris brings a depth and level of emotion to his writing that most authors strive their entire career to achieve, and which many never do.'
Elizabeth A. White - Musings of an All-Purpose Monkey

'Ayris' gripping, gritty, beautiful novel is full of warmth, wit, excitement, comedy and tragedy'
Paul D. Brazill - Author of 13 Shots of Noir

'A fine balance of drama, suspense, and poignancy'
Steve Porter's World of Books

'An amazingly good debut novel.'
Nigel Bird -Author of Smoke

'Fans of films like The Shawshank Redemption will love it.'
Ric's Reviews

'A remarkable first novel'
Naomi Johnson - The Drowning Machine

'An astounding story, with an original voice and style'
Crime Fiction Lover

'A bruising, emotional roller coaster of a read - a remarkable debut novel'
Alan Griffiths - Brit Grit.

'One of the most memorable books I've read in a long time'
Chris Rhatigan - Death By Killing

'An absolute straight-in-the-back-of-the-net knockout of a story'
Jason Michel - Pulp Metal Magazine

'Expect to be moved and taken to a whole different world that is as real as your own'
Eric Beetner - Author of Dig Two Graves

'I absolutely loved 'Abide with Me' and in places was very moved, to both laughter, and tears'
Trevor Drane - Revelation Films

Abide With Me

CHAPTER ONE

There's things happen in your life what go clean out your head. They don't *mean* nothing, see. Most of your life's like that. And there's some things you remember cos they was good and they make you smile even though you know nothing's ever comin back, no matter how hard you wish it. And there's people. Good people. People you won't never see again. People what you loved so much it tears you apart just thinkin of em. It tears you apart cos you know you won't never see that look in their eyes or feel their hand on your shoulder or what it was like just bein with em.

It's all gone, see. And there ain't no way now you can tell em how much you loved em. Not fuckin ever.

But there's other things what happen, other things you don't never wanna remember, cos they hurt. They hurt too fuckin much. And when you close your eyes it's them things what come shoutin and screamin and crawlin out the mist in your head.

Every fuckin time.

***

May 10th Nineteen-seventy-five

Elvis is blarin out Blue Suede Shoes in the front room. Me and Mum's in the kitchen, makin claret and blue paper chains. We got loads of em piled up all over the floor and the table. Bloody loads of em. Dad reckons the house gotta look proper for the match, you know. He's already got em stuck round all the windows, up the tops of the walls, hangin off the ceilin, up the bannisters. Absolutely bleedin everywhere. We been at em since last night, me and Mum, makin em quick as we can, and we got up early to finish off the rest but Dad's stickin em all over the gaff and we can't hardly keep up. He pops his head round the door. His quiff's all fucked and it's hangin over his face like a dead cat. Gives me a wink, he does, and a big thumbs up, grabs handful of paper chains, and he's off.

Fuckin cracks me up, my dad. Mum just ignores him. She don't like it when he starts on the sauce early. Don't like it one bit. Me, I just think it's funny.

We're comin to the end of another lot, me and Mum. Nearly out of sticky tape. Then there's this crash comes out the front room. We both fly in there. Dad's on his arse, paper chains over his head, pissin himself. Thinks it's fuckin hilarious. Mum don't. She's seethin. Her face is all red and everything. But she holds it in. Second time he's come off the ladder this mornin. Silly sod. He'd normally be up for a right bollockin by now, but today's different.

Ten years, see, since the Hammers was at Wembley. Nineteenth of May, nineteen-sixty-five. Cup Winners' Cup Final. Mum and Dad got married the Saturday before, so they was down some caravan at Clacton when the match was on. His mate, Tommy Fuller, he had tickets and everything. Dad watched it in the social club on the site, pissed, Mum reckoned. Yep, he gave up bein at Wembley that day, all for Mum. That's fuckin love, that is. Dad reckons today's the biggest day of his life since then – the match, not marryin Mum – even bigger than when the Hammers won the World Cup in sixty-six.

I know Dad's breakin his neck to get to the game today. I been hearin him and Mum shoutin loads lately, you know, about how tight things is at the minute, so there weren't never no chance he was gettin there. I reckon that's why he's pissed this mornin. So close, you know. So fuckin close.

Mum's holdin the ladder this time, but Dad's nearly come off again. Swayin all over the place, he is, and he's gettin some right filthy looks off Mum. Back steady now. That big grin. I'm layin on the floor, lookin up at him. Wanna get a good look for when he goes next time. He's reachin up, about to hang some paper chains round the light, when he looks down at me, steadies himself, and takes a deep breath like he's about to say something really important.

'Like Christmas in claret, this is, son,' he says, startin to sway. 'Christmas in bleedin claret.'

Makes no fuckin sense to me, if I'm honest, but Dad says it like he's Winston bloody Churchill.

Mum shakes her head at him slow, raises her eyebrows and rolls her eyes all in one hit. Makes me smile cos when she does that, I know she loves him more than anything in the whole world.

***

By kick-off, the house is packed. Mum, Dad, me, Nan and Grandad, Auntie Ivy, Auntie Gwen. Me uncle, Uncle Derek, he's Spurs and Dad won't have him in the house. Not on a day like this. Fuckin fair enough, when you think about it.

Auntie Gwen's brought me round a claret and blue scarf she's knitted special and Auntie Ivy's done some fairy cakes with claret and blue icing. The cakes look fuckin ropey, tell you the truth, but they're all gone by the time Bonzo's leadin the lads out at quarter to three.

Nan and Grandad's sittin on the settee and Mum's on the arm, ready to jump up to make a cuppa at a moment's fuckin notice. Nan used to be the same till she got ill. Now she don't hardly move at all. Auntie Ivy's on her knees behind Nan and Grandad, pokin her face out the top of the settee, and me Auntie Gwen's in the other armchair, suckin on a fag. I'm about two foot from the telly. I got me light blue school shirt on and me mauve tank-top, and me heart's beatin ten to the fuckin dozen inside. Dad's behind me. In his armchair. I've just looked round, and he's sittin there like he's plugged into the fuckin mains.

'John?' Mum says. 'Where's Becky?'

I know Becky's me little sister and all that, and I love her to bits. But fuck me, she's hard work.

'She's over here, dear,' Auntie Ivy says, holdin her up from behind the settee.

Little mare's got a mouthful of paper chains. Auntie Ivy ain't got a clue, but Mum's see em.

'Becky!' she says. 'Take them out of your mouth right this instant.'

Becky gives Mum one of her big grins. She looks just like Dad when she does that, like what he does when Mum's tellin him off when he's pissed.

'You naughty girl,' Auntie Ivy says, pullin the paper out of Becky's mouth and holdin her close at the same time. She rubs her nose on Becky's, both of em gigglin, and puts her down so we can all go back to the telly.

The players are all lined up now. Some Duke of fuckin somewhere's goin along the line shakin hands with em.

Mum pipes up again.

'Who's he, dear?' she says.

Mum likes to know things like that, you know, useless shit what don't mean fuck all. But Dad don't answer. He's in a world of his own.

The bloke on the telly's goin on about Bobby Moore bein captain of Fulham after all them years at West Ham. I can hear me dad whisperin behind me, choked, like it's right from his heart, you know.

'You'll always be an 'ammer, son,' he's sayin. 'Always a fuckin 'ammer.'

I look round. Dad's got his eyes bulgin like they're gonna burst out his head and his knuckles have gone all white where he's holdin on to the arms of the chair so hard.

The whistle goes. Dad goes bang.

'COME ON YOU FUCKIN IRONS.'

'Bill!'

But Dad ain't takin no notice of Mum. He don't mean it. Can't help it. Like he says, this is the biggest day of his life for ten years, and he ain't gonna smooth off the edges for no one. Not even Mum.

Dad don't stop screamin and swearin till the final whistle. Fulham's much better than us first half, and we all know it. We're a division above em and should be strollin it, but they've got guts they have. And they've got Bobby Moore. We sneak a couple of goals in the second half from Alan Taylor, and win two-nil. Fuckin lucky, if you ask me. I'm watchin Bobby Moore goin round shakin hands with the West Ham players at the end of the game, head held high, stridin. And I'm thinkin, that's a real hero. I got a lump in me throat and I got no idea why. Not really. Thought Dad'd be jumpin all over the place by now, up and down like Auntie Ivy and Auntie Gwen, but when I look round, he's just sittin there. Not a sound. And I know he's been watchin Bobby Moore, same as me.

But when the West Ham players start climbin the steps to get the cup, it starts. A sort of low murmur behind me, strained through gritted teeth, like a shit ventriloquist.

'I'm forever blowin bubbles, pretty bubbles in the air.'

There's tears comin down his face and there's car horns soundin outside, cheerin and shoutin and yellin and whoopin from kids runnin down the street.

'They fly so high, nearly reach the sky, then like my dreams they fade and die.'

Fantastic.

Bonzo's liftin the cup, and I got this tinglin all over, like I got a little bit of what Dad's feelin. I look round at him again, and he's stood up clappin with the hundreds and thousands of other Hammers in the ground. He's got the biggest smile you ever see, and them tears are still runnin down his face.

Then he starts singin again. This time, top of his voice, arms up.

'FORTUNE'S ALWAYS HIDIN, I'VE LOOKED
EVERYWHERE, I'M FOREVER BLOWING BUBBLES,
PRETTY BUBBLES IN THE AIR.'

Becky waddles up to Dad and he picks her up under his arm.

'Come on, son,' he says to me, and picks me up under the other arm like I'm light as a fuckin feather. Becky's squealin, and Dad's marchin us out to the front door like he's got the strength of a

4

thousand men. When he gets out in the hall he stops cos he ain't got no more hands left to open the front door. Silly bugger. Mum comes out in the hall after us, fearin he's gonna drop us all, squeezes past, and lets us out.

***

Street's fuckin teemin. Front doors wide open, people singin, slappin each other on the back, huggin each other. Bubbles everywhere. Even Old Cartwright next door – a miserable bastard at the best of fuckin times – is kitted out in an old Hammers scarf. Claret and blue. Him and his scarf, faded to fuck.

Dad puts me and Becky down, cos he's fuckin knackered, and starts jabberin with Old Cartwright.

Every house in the street's got some sort of West Ham on it, banners, flags, all sorts of shit. All other than the house opposite, they ain't got fuck all. That's the new people. Moved in a couple weeks back. Ain't seen nothing of em, meself, but Mum says the woman's friendly enough.

So here's me, holdin Becky's hand, wonderin why the new people's house ain't got nothing up, when the front door opens and this fat kid comes tumblin out, door slammin behind him. He don't even try and get back in. Just sits on the front step and puts his hands over his ears and closes his eyes. He's got on these grey trousers and white shirt, and he's wearin shoes, and even a fuckin tie. Cup Final day, and he's all got up in his bleedin school uniform. Gotta be some kind of fuckin idiot, obviously.

Dad's still talkin to Old Cartwright, and I'm lookin at this fat kid sittin on the step, sittin like he's shut the whole fuckin world out. I leave Becky holdin onto Dad's legs and go over. The kid's got his hands over his face now, and when I get close, I see he's got blood comin through his fingers and his whole body's shakin.

'You all right, mate?' I says.

He turns his back on me and don't say a word.

'Just askin, that's all,' I says.

Fuckin arsehole.

I sit down on the step next to him. He don't move a muscle, just sits there with his back to me. And then I hear this racket goin on in the house like you wouldn't fuckin believe. Shoutin and crashin and breakin, and shit.

After a while, Dad comes over.

'I'm off down the boozer, son,' he says. 'Tell your mother for us.'

It's like Dad ain't even see the fat kid next to me. Like the kid ain't even there.

Dad come home two days later after he'd pissed all his wages up the wall. Mum had him in the fuckin doghouse ages for pullin that stunt.

The last few weeks of school fly by. Summer's the same. Every day, me and Dad, over the park, doin the Cup Final all over. When September rolls round, I'm in a new class at school.

And there's this empty seat sittin right next to me.

CHAPTER TWO

Miss Felton. The lovely Miss Felton. Big brown eyes, blonde hair. Face like a baboon's arse.

'Morning, children.'

'Mornin, Miss.'

At ten or eleven, you think you know how things is gonna turn out. You think you know fuckin everything, but you know fuck all, really.

'Right then, everyone. Settle down, please. Thank you.'

'Lisa Cross?'

Nice girl. Chucked herself off Waterloo Bridge at nineteen. Fuckin tragic.

'Here, Miss.'

'George Somerton?'

Road sweeper. Born to push a fuckin broom, that boy.

See, it's always been a shit-hole, Bethnal Green. That's what me dad always reckoned. Always was a shit-hole and always fuckin will be. Only way you make it out, he said, was if you was a boxer or a gangster. Ronnie or Reggie or John H. Stracey. Take your fuckin pick. No? Well, best of bleedin luck.

'Jimmy Lawson?'

Crackhead. Tosser.

'Absent, Miss.'

'Thank you, Susan. Alison Bennet?'

Shelf stacker. Stacks shelves.

'Here, Miss.'

'Steven Dobbs?'

Nutter. Doin a ten stretch in Parkhurst for drivin a stolen motor through Woolies. Maimed twelve.

'Yes, Miss.'

'Johnny Sissons?'

That's me.

'Yes, Miss.'

And as she's readin out the names, goin down the list, I'm sittin here thinkin not a one of us has got a fuckin chance, you know. Not a fuckin hope. I'm thinkin this, when the fat kid from over the road knocks on the classroom door.

Miss Felton comes across and lets him in.

'You must be Kenneth,' she says.

He nods his head, but he don't say a fuckin word or nothing. Miss Felton says for him to sit next to me.

Like I says, the age we was then, you think you know everything. But what you don't know, what you ain't got a clue about, is when the whole world turns to shit and you think there ain't no fuckin way out . . .

'Harry Wilkins?'

'Yes, Miss.'

. . . there's someone gonna come along and turn the whole fuckin place upside down.

'Kenneth Montgomery?'

'Present, Miss.'

***

That first day in class, Kenny come in with a busted lip. He come in with pretty much everything after that. Black eyes, cuts, bruises, all sorts of shit. Cos of it, Miss Felton'd talk different to Kenny than what she did the rest of us. Sort of kinder, you know. Always askin if he's all right. Never says he ain't, never gives nothing away, does Kenny. She gives him that lovely smile of hers and moves on. Never pushes it, she don't. It's like she thinks he's gonna break or something.

Wilkins pokes me in the back. He's always tappin me for something, that leechin bastard.

'Johnny,' he says, 'you got a spare pencil, mate? I've left mine at 'ome.'

I shake me head. I've only got one that ain't broke at the end, and I ain't givin him that. Next to me, Kenny's got this sort of writin set out. Metal case and everything. Two pencils, rubber, ruler, and a fuckin fountain pen, would you believe. None of us got one of them. He's writin the date in his exercise book, tongue out the side of his mouth like he's really concentratin. Eighth of September nineteen-seventy-five.

Big black letters at the top of the page.

'Oi, Fatty?' Wilkins says. 'Give us one of them pencils.'

I tell Wilkins to fuck off, and give him a look so he knows I ain't messin. Kenny's sittin dead still, lookin forward, like he ain't heard nothing, but I know he has cos the fountain pen in his hand's shakin on the side of the metal tin.

I start turnin round to give Wilkins another mouthful, when Miss Felton spots us. Asks if we're all right. I tell her Wilkins has forgot his pencil.

'Thank you, John,' she says, and tells Wilkins to go and get a pencil off her.

'Yes, Miss,' he says.

Wilkins pushes Kenny in the head when he goes past him and whispers something in his ear. Kenny goes all red, and Wilkins goes up to get his pencil. Horrible fucker, Wilkins.

'Now, children. I'd like you to open your desks and take out your maths books, please. We'll begin the year with a little test.'

Groans. Desk lids creak up and down. Pencils clatter on the floor. Someone farts. That'll be Lenny Thompson – Thommo. My best mate. Filthy fucker, he is. Everyone laughs, the boys anyway. Not the girls. A fuckin maths test is serious shit to them, and they give us some right old looks. I look across at Kenny. He's sittin up straight, pencil in his hand, tongue out the side of his mouth like before, ready to start.

'That'll do, children. Lenny, do have some manners, please.'

'Yes, Miss.'

'Now, complete this test in silence, as best you can everyone. Thank you. Okay. Number one. Eighteen plus fifty-seven.'

Pencils scratch. Thommo lets one off again. Sniggers all round. Miss Felton can't be bothered with him no more, and carries on with the test.

'Number two. Ninety-six minus twenty-five.'

I get four out of twenty. Not bad, for me. Kenny gets two. Bottom of the class. And he gets this big smile on his face when Miss Felton tells him, like he don't even know how fuckin stupid he is. All dressed up in his la-de-da and he's thicker than the fuckin lot of us. And as she's talkin to him, Miss Felton, he's got his head down already, writin tomorrow's date on the next page. No doubt in my mind there's something wrong with the geezer. No fuckin doubt at all. Knows his days, though, I give him that.

But he stood out the day he walked in, Kenny did. There's the rest of us, shirts hangin out, trainers, hair not washed for days, and there's him with his white shirts and shiny shoes, and this flowery fuckin tie round his neck. Ain't like he's even gotta wear it. Not part of the school uniform or nothing. Gets peanutted more times than I can count, he does, but he never takes the fuckin thing off. Poor bastard gets his fair share of kick-ins an all. I do me best lookin out for him, you know, best I can, but it's like he's fuckin askin for it what with dressin like that and bein so fuckin dopey. I mean, for fuck's sake.

***

It's me birthday come end of October. I'm about the oldest in our year, other than Lindsey Rogers, of course. She always brings a load of sweets in when it's her birthday. That's why I remember that. I have all me birthdays over The Barmy, loads of mates, kickin a ball about. And this one ain't no different.

But on this birthday, for some reason I ain't got no fuckin clue about, Mum makes me invite Kenny. She says it's only right, seein as he lives across the street an that, and I sit next to him in class. Kenny don't seem too keen on the idea when I tell him, to be fair. But he turns up anyway, in his bloody shirt and shoes and tie get-up, mind. Fuckin idiot.

***

Park's empty. Fuckin brilliant. No one wants Kenny on their team, but Dad puts him on ours anyway. We stick him in goal, get him out the way, you know.

Robbie Jenkins won't take his coat off for a post, not even when I ask him nice and tell him it's me birthday. He says he don't care. Reckons his mum'll kill him if he gets his coat dirty, so we gotta move the pitch up the slope and use this big fuck off tree for one of the posts. Seems a good idea at the time, till Robbie slides his leg right across the side of it tryin to clear one off the line. Cuts his knee right open. Has to go back to my house with his jumper wrapped round his leg to stop the blood pissin out. Serves him fuckin right, I reckon.

We're a man short, cos of Robbie, but none of us care. We play on for hours, till it gets dark and none of us can see fuck all. Dad's ref. I score loads and Kenny's shit. Got no fuckin idea. He won't dive or nothing. Kitted out like a fuckin waiter I don't suppose he was ever gonna anyway. He can't even catch a ball. Only time he kicks it, the silly bastard falls flat on his arse. Even Dad laughs at that one. A couple of times, Kenny gets the ball right in the face. And he never even fuckin flinched.

Back home, Mum tells us all to go up and wash our hands. There's about ten of us, so it's a bit of a stampede. Kenny's standin in the hall waitin for the rest of us so he can go up.

When we go in the front room, Dad's set up the wallpaper table and Mum's chucked a tablecloth on it and filled her best

Tupperware with jam sandwiches, chocolate fingers, crisps – mostly twisters, cos I love them – plastic beakers full of Cherryade, and a plate of marshmallow teacakes. They're Becky's favourites. After we've stuffed all that, Mum dishes up the jelly and ice-cream. After that, she brings out this big fuck-off trifle with loads of hundreds and thousands on it. Knows how to do a party, my mum. Kenny gets a bit of stick when the trifle comes out, but Mum says anyone who carries on can go home. That stops it. We ain't a bad lot, you know, just kids, that's all.

***

Was a couple months later, headin for Christmas, when Mum tells me I'm goin round Kenny's for tea. Says she bumped into his mum in Sainsbury's and his mum tells her what a great time Kenny had at me party and that she'd love to have me round, or some such bollocks. That day at school, Kenny never says nothing. Not one fuckin word. Then, when the bell goes at the end of the last lesson, he says to me about it. Don't look too fuckin chuffed neither. Sort of embarrassed, like. Can't say I'm over the fuckin moon meself, lookin at the state of his face every fuckin day.

We walk out the gates together, and he goes left instead of right. I ask him where he's goin. He tells me he's goin the long way round.

When we get to his house I see the nets in the front room move. Kenny's mum opens the door before we get to the house and comes scurryin out. Holds him right tight to her. Kenny, he's stiff as a board. When she lets him go he legs it in the house and I can hear him peltin straight up the stairs. His mum looks over at me.

'Hello, you must be John,' she says.

Posh bird. Can't be from round here. Loads of make-up an all, looks like one of them fuckin mannykin things in the shops. And she's got this hurry-up look on her like she don't wanna be leavin Kenny too long in the house on his own.

'I've heard so much about you,' she says, and hurries me inside.

I wonder if the old man's about. By the look on the old girl's face, and how Kenny's shot up them stairs, I reckon he probably is.

CHAPTER THREE

Kenny's mum says for me to come through. First thing I notice, there ain't no doors. Where the front room is, the back room, the kitchen – all through the passage, it's just empty doorways. She shows me in the front room, tells me Kenny won't be long. Carpet's this horrible sort of brown and orange colour. Mind you, it's like the whole fuckin world's brown and orange these days; our curtains – all of em, Nan's carpet, Auntie Ivy's shoes, Auntie Ivy herself, when she's had a day at Southend. Bloody everything. It's tidier than our gaff round here, but sort of empty. No photos on the wall like what we got over our place, no pictures, no papers, no comics all everywhere, no shit all over the floor like Becky's toys. I can't even see no telly. There's just a couple of armchairs, a wooden seat by where the door should be, and a three-bar electric fire. And that's off. Fuckin freezin in here, it is.

And there he is. Kenny's old man. Asleep in this tatty armchair in the corner, snorin like a fuckin warthog.

Kenny's mum says she'll get me a drink and some biscuits, sort of whisperin, lookin over her shoulder at the old man all the time, like she don't wanna wake him up for the fuckin world.

The old man's a weedy lookin fucker. String vest, army trousers. All of it filthy. And he's got these tattoos all up his arms and over his knuckles. Stinks of booze. Fuckin reeks of it.

I sit down on the wooden seat by the door.

Kenny's mum goes, backin out the door, not takin her eyes off him the whole fuckin time. Comes back a minute later with a beaker of juice and a couple of Custard Creams, by which time I've nearly gone and fuckin shit meself, I'm so scared.

She's nice, Kenny's mum. But the old man, it's like sittin in a cage with a sleepin fuckin lion. She asks me if I'm in Kenny's class at school, even though she knows I am.

I nod me head, mouth full of biscuits.

Fuck. The old man's wakin up. He's snufflin and yawnin and he's got his eyes half open and he's lookin straight at me.

'Who the fuck are you?' he says, right fuckin angry.

Eyes like piss-holes in the snow, he's got. He's scarin the shit right out of me, I can fuckin tell you.

Kenny's mum, she tells him, all shaky, I'm a friend of Kenny's, come round for tea. Hearin her say Kenny's name, his eyes go all black. Tells her he wants to know where Kenny is. Calls him a fat bastard. Never takes his eyes off me, though, he don't, long as he's talkin. Not for one fuckin second. Kenny's mum don't like him callin Kenny a fat bastard, and she tells him, but she's twice as fuckin scared as me.

'I said,' he says, his voice getting louder and harder, 'where is that fat fuckin bastard?'

Tears come in her eyes, and she gets up and goes. She fuckin goes. Fuck. I wet meself a bit and hope it don't show, and I drink me juice, just to have something to hide behind. I drink it down in one hit, and when I look up, the old man's gone asleep again. I take me chances, and sneak out in the hall quiet as I can.

Like I says, there ain't no doors down here, so I see right through to the kitchen. Kenny's mum's wipin her eyes and butterin some bread. I've half a mind to leg it out the front door right there and fuckin then, but she clocks me and gives me this sort of 'please fuckin stay' smile. I smile back, sort of simple, like, and look at the floor. I've really gotta have a piss proper, so I start up the stairs, hopin to fuck they don't creak.

***

It's dark up the stairs. No lights. I reckon the toilet's the room on the right at the top, cos it's got a door, and it's where ours is at home. I do me business and come out, rememberin to wash me hands like Mum always says. The room next to the toilet's got no door, like downstairs, and it's all dark. I take a peek. Double bed, all nicely made up. There's a light comin under the door the other side of the landin. Only other door in the house, lookin at it, other than the shit-house. Gotta be Kenny's gaff. I make me way over. The stairs was all right, but the landin, the landin creaks like fuck. I know Kenny's heard me cos I can hear him movin about inside and there's a shadow movin across the bottom of the door and back again.

Kenny's mum shouts up tea's ready. Well, she don't shout, exactly, more sort of like whispers really loud, like Mum does when she's tellin me off somewhere quiet like the library or the Doctor's or something. That sort of whisper everyone can hear, you know.

I'm waitin for Kenny. But he ain't comin out. I look over the bannisters, and his mum's waitin for us. I knock on Kenny's door, tell him tea's ready. The bed squeaks where he gets off, and he opens the door a crack. Room smells of piss and the floorboards ain't got nothing on em. Poor bastard.

I tell him again, tea's ready, but he don't say nothing, just comes out. He don't even look at me. We go downstairs and follow his mum into the back room where she's got tea on the table.

She says for me to sit down, pointin at the chair opposite where Kenny's gone and sat, and tells me to help meself to whatever I want.

There's jam sarnies, crisps – plain, not Twisters or Wotsits or nothing fancy like that – a plate of Custard Creams and chocolate Bourbons all mixed together, and a jug of lemonade. Kenny's mum pours some of the lemonade out for us. Kenny's already pilin up his plate.

I'm in the middle of leanin over for a Bourbon when Kenny's old man weasels in. Everything stops. He sits down next to me, opposite Kenny's mum. She asks him if he wants a drink and holds up the bottle of lemonade. I'm shittin meself all over.

He picks up the plate of jam sarnies and looks at her like she's gone off her nut.

'What the fuck are *these*?' he says, holdin the plate under her nose. '*Jam sandwiches? Jam fuckin sandwiches*?' He don't stop. 'You call this fuckin tea?' he says. Then he Frisbees the whole thing against the wall. Jam sarnies and bits of plate all over the gaff.

Then he turns on Kenny. Leans over the table. Right in close. Tells Kenny to clear it up.

Kenny just sits there, head down, lookin at his plate. *Come on Kenny*, I'm thinkin. *Come on*. Just do what the fucker says. But he don't. Just carries on sittin there. The old man, he ain't havin none of that. He leans right over this time, grabs the back of Kenny's hair and pulls his head right back till Kenny's lookin at the ceiling.

'I said, pick em up, you fat, lazy, fuckin cunt,' he says.

Then he gobs in Kenny's face and pushes his head back so hard he comes off the chair. Next thing, Kenny's on the floor pickin up jam sarnies and bits of plate. But he ain't doin it quick. He's doin it like he's got all the time in the fuckin world.

It's all gone up a level now. The old man's really fuckin losin it.

'That's it, little porky, on your fat fuckin belly,' he says. 'You fat fuckin piece of shit.'

There's tears comin down Kenny's mum's face now. But she's just sittin there an all. Like Kenny did. I think about helpin Kenny out, but I'm shittin meself, and I can't take me eyes off the old man cos I dunno where he's goin next. Then Kenny's mum says something. Big fuckin mistake, that is. Tells the old man to pack it in. Hardly more than a whisper, like it's all she's got left.

'You what?' he says. 'You say something? You fuckin say something?'

Then he bangs her right in the face. Proper punch an all, like he's hittin a geezer. And I piss meself proper this time. Kenny's old girl falls back against the wall, holdin her face, blood pissin through her fingers. Then the old man plonks himself down in his seat, puts his head in his hands, and starts sobbin like a fuckin baby. Kenny's still crawlin round the floor pickin up jam sarnies and bits of plate, and me, I can't move cos I been froze to me seat the whole fuckin time.

***

And that was tea at Kenny's. I didn't tell Mum nothing. Said I pissed meself on the way home from school. She says not to worry, and gives me a kiss on the head. That's when I started bawlin me eyes out.

Come night-time, I'm lyin in me bed. Can't sleep. Been tryin to close me eyes for ages, but soon as I do, I see Kenny's old man cryin his heart out and Kenny shufflin about the floor pickin up jam sarnies, and all over there's the sound of his old girl screamin.

***

Mum and Dad's downstairs. Mum's laughin. Probably something on the telly or Dad's told her one of his stupid jokes, something he'd picked up in the factory or out the boozer. Becky's movin about in her cot like she can't sleep neither. She's breathin heavy, sort of two at a time, like she's cryin. But she's not. It's just how she gets sometimes.

Can't get Kenny out me head still, thinkin about him across the road, tryin to get to sleep. And I'm thinkin what I'd do if I was him. I know I wouldn't fuckin be puttin up with it, that's for fuckin starters. I'd be workin out how to have it away on me toes first thing, like that Dick Whittinton geezer. I'd do the old man in before I went, an all. Get a gun or something. Blow the bastard's head off.

The stairs start creakin. Door opens. Mum comes in to check on Becky, and I squeeze me eyes tight shut. I can hear Mum whisperin to Becky and singin soft, probably strokin her hair and her cheek, an that. She's right gentle, Mum. Then I can hear her footsteps comin over to me. I close me eyes even tighter. Don't wanna talk about what's in me head, you know, doin away with Kenny's old man. Mum feels me forehead, and gives me a kiss there. Then she gets a tissue and she's wipin me eyes and she's wipin the tears off me face. She cups her hand round me cheek, and I know she's lookin right into me. Gives me another kiss on the forehead and I know I'm cryin now cos I can hear it in me throat. But I won't open me eyes, not even for Mum. I'm willin for her to go. And when she does, when the bedroom door shuts tight and the lights go out, I want her back all over again, just so she can stop the screamin in me head.

***

As for Kenny, next day at school, all week, I got an empty fuckin chair sittin next to me.

CHAPTER FOUR

The week Kenny's off, Miss Felton starts sortin out the Christmas play. She does her best, bless her, but it was always gonna be a fuckin disaster.

Like I says, Miss Felton, she's lovely and all that, but she ain't got no fuckin idea. Not really. Like havin Steve Luxford talkin out front last year. Thought it'd give him confidence, she did. Steve fuckin Luxford. Poor fucker had a stutter on him like someone's jumpin on his throat. Tore him to bits, talkin out front. Poor bastard ain't never been the same since. So when it's just who plays Joseph left, and there's only Kenny's left over, it weren't like I fuckin fell off me chair or nothing.

Rachel Johnson – she's Mary – she's in bits, Wilkins is pissin himself, and half the class is in fuckin uproar. Me, I'm just thinkin of Kenny. Poor fuck.

***

When I get home, I tell Mum I need a tea-towel.

'What for, love?'

I tell her it's cos I'm gonna be a shepherd in the play, and she goes off rummagin in the kitchen drawers. Turns the kitchen half upside down, she does. I tell her I gotta have one. It's what they wore in them days. In the end, she finds one down the side of the cooker with tractors and shit on it, something Auntie Ivy bought back from Suffolk a couple years back.

'I'll give it a wash, love,' she says, 'get the beans out. It'll come up good as new.'

I don't give a fuck about the beans. Long as I got a tea-towel.

Then Mum makes me up one of them dress things what the geezers wore in the Bible out of an old sheet, and gets one of Nan's old walkin sticks and tapes up a load of toilet rolls on the bottom to make it longer. I paint it brown with some paint out the shed, and Bob's your fuckin Uncle. I'm all sorted.

But I know Kenny ain't got a fuckin hope of gettin hold of nothing round his gaff. So Mum knocks up a dress for him, and cuts up another bit of sheet to stick on his head. She gets me to try my gear on and takes me in the front room to show Dad.

'Very nice, son,' he says. 'Very nice.' Then he pulls the telly paper in front of his face so I can't see him laughin.

Mum gives Dad one of her filthy looks, and I get me shepherd kit off right there and fuckin then.

***

Kenny's back at school next week. Don't look too bad. Nothing obvious, like. Wilkins can't wait.

'Oi, Fatty,' he says.

Kenny turns round in his seat.

'Find yourself a tea-towel, mate. You're gonna be a shepherd.'

Kenny looks at him blank.

'That's right, mate. Bloody good part, that is.'

What an horrible fucker.

I don't wanna tell Kenny he's Joseph. Turns out, I don't have to. Miss Felton comes over quick as you like, and gives him the play and all his lines coloured in. Kenny has a quick look, and his face goes white. Looks like he's gonna chuck his breakfast up over his shoes.

'Don't worry, Kenneth,' she says. 'I'll help you through it.'

Quick smile, and leaves him for dead. Not a fuckin clue.

'You'll be all right,' I says. 'You can practice round my house, if you want.'

And it's like he's lookin at me and through me and past me all at the same time, like he's a million fuckin miles away. And there's these tears in his eyes. Like glue. And tears like that, they don't never fall.

Wilkins pokes me in the back with his pencil.

'You turnin fuckin ginger or something, Sissons?'

I turn round quick, snap his pencil in half and tell him to fuck off.

'All right, Johnny, mate, all right. Only messin.'

Bastard.

***

Kenny never did come round to practice. But I walk home every day with him, and we do it then. I do his part and he says it back. He's really slow to start, like he can't hardly read, but he starts gettin it a little bit at a time. To be honest, he ain't got much. And with Miss Felton sittin with him most days, I'm startin to think he might fuckin be okay, you know.

But ever since the parts was dished out, Wilkins got it right in for

Kenny. Rips the arse out of him every fuckin day. Kenny don't look like he's takin much notice. Don't even turn round most times. And I'm thinkin nutty old Miss Felton might have actually done the fuckin trick this time. But when the big day comes, Kenny's fuckin brickin it. He's sittin on a bale of hay at the back of the stage behind the curtain, shakin. Mumblin to himself, he is. All sorts of bollocks. Keeps gettin up and lookin round the curtain at all the empty seats. In the end, Miss Felton tells him to sit down and has a quiet word with him.

I look round the side of the stage just before we're about to kick off, and half the seats is empty. Mum and Dad's here, with Becky. Becky's got her own chair. Bet she's lovin that. Big smile on her face. Can't see Kenny's mum, not less she's late. Never thought the old man would turn up, but thought the old girl might make an effort. When I come back round the curtain, Kenny's lookin at me, you know, like he knows she ain't comin. Gets to a time when you're sort of expectin it, I suppose.

'Right then, children. Places, please.'

Here we go.

Miss Felton's in a worse state than the rest of us. Shakin all over she is. She's already snapped at Thommo a couple of times for pullin cotton wool balls off the sheep, and Jimmy Lawson for nudgin Rachel Johnson off a bale of hay.

'Miss? Miss?'

It's Rachel Johnson. Again.

'Yes, Rachel. What is it this time?'

Rachel's proper blubbin. In a right state, she is.

'Miss, someone took the baby Jesus, Miss.'

Miss Felton swears under her breath, and it's sort of funny to see. And while everyone's lookin for the Son of God, I see Jimmy Lawson put him back in the shoe-box manger thing and cover him up with straw.

'Here it is, Miss,' Jimmy says, all helpful, like.

'Well done, Jimmy. Now Rachel, calm down, dear. That's enough crying. Everything is going to be all right.'

It's like she's almost talkin to herself when she says that last bit.

Miss Felton claps her hands twice. 'Shepherds? Sheep? Places!' And she disappears on stage.

I hear a couple of people clappin, and she comes back. Looks like she needs a fuckin drink.

'Okay, children. Off you go.'

I lead the shepherds out, and the sheep come on behind us.

'Go on, son.'

It's Dad, standin up, wavin at me. He's got that big grin on his face, and just seein it makes me smile. Can't look at him long, though, cos I'll start laughin. Mum does one of her loud whispers in his ear that everyone can hear, and he does this pretend told off thing what he does, you know, like Droopy off the cartoons.

And you know what, it's all goin un-fuckin-believable. Everyone's spot on with their lines, there's no one fallin off the stage like little Charlie Hammond last year, and even Kenny's goin like a dream.

It's near the end, and we're all on stage now. Shepherds, kings, Mary and Joseph, farm animals. Everyone. I'm close to it all, right near the shoe-box manger thing. One of the perks of bein Head Shepherd, that is. Jimmy Lawson tips me a wink. Shit.

'Dear Mary,' Jimmy says, like he's Laurence fuckin Oliver. 'Please let us see the face of our Lord.'

Without thinkin, cos I mean, it ain't in the lines or nothing, but it's a fair fuckin request, you know, Rachel Johnson scrapes the straw off the face of the Son of God. And, fuck me, he's got two red Smarties in his eyes and a fag hangin out his mouth.

Rachel screams. The Three Kings are in fits, and the sheep are all over the place. Miss Felton runs on the stage, puts her arm round Rachel, and tries calmin her down.

Fuckin chaos.

And then there's Kenny. My mate, Kenny. Bein Joseph, he's been sat next to Rachel Johnson the whole time. He ain't moved a muscle. Never even flinched when she broke in half after seein what Lawson did to the baby Jesus. Just sat there, he did. And he's still sittin there, starin out at the crowd, sort of squintin, like he's tryin to see something, like there's something out there he just can't make out. I've stopped me laughin cos I can't take me eyes off him. And now he's standin up and he's movin towards the front of the stage, right through the middle of everything.

Stops right at the edge of the stage, he does. Right at the front. Thought he was gonna throw himself off for a second, you know, something really mad like that, but from the way the crowd's lookin at him it's like he's talkin to them or something. Can't hear proper what he's sayin cos of the shoutin and the cryin and World War fuckin Three goin off all round me, but whatever he's sayin, every fuckin head in the crowd's takin notice. Mum's dabbin away the tears off her face with a hanky, and Dad's like the rest, can't take his eyes off Kenny.

Back here, Rachel Johnson's finally stopped her cryin, the shepherds and the kings and the sheep have stopped laughin, and we're all just sittin quiet, listenin to Kenny. But we're too late to hear much of anything, cos he's just finished. I know he's finished cos Dad's stood up and started clappin. And he ain't the only one. Every fucker in the hall's gettin up. One, two at a time, the whole lot cheerin. The blokes are clappin like at football, you know, hands over your head, and the women have all got their tissues out. Miss Felton's gone up front with Kenny and she's cuddlin him to her. I get up on a bale of hay and start clappin meself. Lenny does the same. And before you know it, the whole class is givin it up for Kenny and whatever the fuck he's just done. Everyone other than Lawson, that is. He fucked off sharpish soon as Kenny stopped talkin.

Kenny's had his back to us the whole time he's up there, so I never see him proper. But Mum said the way he walked forward and told em the rest of the story of Jesus bein born and the star and the angels, and that, she said it was like it was happenin right in front of him. And when he finished, and everyone started clappin, she said the smile he had on his face was one of the most beautiful things she ever see.

CHAPTER FIVE

Every Christmas I get a pillow case at the end of me bed, stuffed full. Nothing much, you know, bars of chocolate, colourin books, socks, 'Roy of the Rovers' annual. Things like that. This year I wake up – nothing. I check under the bed. I get out and feel in the corner of the room. I check under the bed again. Still fuckin nothing.

I try and get back to sleep but there's no way that's gonna happen. Can't believe it. Not even a fuckin orange. Dad hears me cryin. Must do, cos he comes in, big smile on his face, wearin a Santa hat. Silly bastard. Big kid, really, he is. A big fuckin kid.

'Happy Christmas, son,' he says, sort of slurrin.

He's a bit too loud, and Becky starts movin about. She's been waitin up all night, bless her. Wanted to hear Santa's bells. I stopped believin long time back, but I make an effort for Mum and Dad. Still pretend, you know. Like I always keep me eyes shut when Dad comes in ringin his little hand bell, the one he got off Brick Lane. Sounds just like Santa's bells, so it does the job. Just for a laugh, he sometimes rings it when he wants Mum to make him a cuppa and she gives him a look and tells him to make it his bloody self.

Dad bends down to pick Becky up out her cot, and his Santa hat falls on her head. They're both gigglin, Dad and Becky. Clear Dad's been drinkin already, just by the sound of him. Not just Santa's glass of milk neither, I should reckon. Never rough with the booze, though, my dad. Not like Kenny's bastard of an old man. A bit silly, that's all, like bein a bit braver with Mum, you know, takin the piss out her cookin and stuff, all jokin, like. Then he falls asleep in his chair and we have to wake him for tea. That's his usual performance.

I'm still gutted about the present thing, but seein Dad cheers me up. And I can smell bacon comin from downstairs. Fuck the smell of pine forests and all that shit on the adverts off the telly. Rip open your presents, then it's bacon sarnies and a cuppa. That's a proper fuckin Christmas, that is.

'Got something for you downstairs, son.'

With the bedroom door open, it's gettin bloody cold in here. I wrap me blankets round me, still tryin to work out what's goin on with me presents.

'Come on, son.'

***

Dad's carryin Becky over his shoulder now, on his way out the bedroom. Becky's smilin at me like she knows what's goin on. Littl'uns are funny like that. See the world, they do. The lights are off on the landin, so the stairs are all dark. And when we get in the front room, there's only the light comin under the kitchen door that shows anything. I can hear Mum shufflin about in there, and the bacon sizzlin on the stove.

'Bill, stoke the fire up, love. And get some jumpers for the kids.'

It's the same voice Mum shouts at me and Becky when she's tellin us something we gotta do. And she don't change it for Dad. Talks to him like that most of the time. Nothing in it, it's just the way they talk, I suppose. And when Dad's like this, you know, a bit tipsy, it's like she's got three fuckin kids anyway. Jokes about it with me two aunties, she does, when they're about, but sometimes she sounds so tired when she says it.

I squeeze past Dad at the bottom of the stairs and go straight in the front room. Can't see nothing cos the fire ain't givin out no light. Dad puts Becky down and she waddles over and wraps her arms round me legs, then Dad comes over and starts pokin round the grate a bit. When the fire starts catchin, he goes upstairs to get our jumpers. Stumbles up the first step, he does. Half pissed. Don't reckon Mum knows how much he's had. Comes out the kitchen, though, see what all the noise is about. The light from where she's opened the door makes it a bit easier to see, but fuck, I still don't see nothing like presents. Heart's beatin fast. Eyes fillin up.

Becky goes over to Mum, and Mum sits her on her knee. Dad's back. Stumbles down the last step and tries to cover it up by doin a little jump at the end.

'Bill! You'll wake up Mr Cartwright!'

'Sorry, dear.'

Dad winks at me when Mum's got her radar off him, and chucks our jumpers over. I put mine on then help Becky with hers. Then he turns on the light and there's two pillow cases, stuffed full, sittin on the settee. Thank fuck. It's Becky's first real Christmas. She knows one of em's hers, and tries draggin the nearest one off the settee.

'Bill, take that off her. That one's John's.'

Dad wrestles the pillow case off Becky. She ain't happy and goes runnin over to Mum. Mum cuddles her up and Dad chucks her pillow case over and she dives on it. I lump me pillow case on the floor, and get me presents out one at a time. Becky's already tearin the paper off hers.

There's more than normal this year. Mum's been takin in more ironin of late, and Dad's never come home till after seven from the factory last couple months. I stack me presents in a pile. I'll open em later, when no one's lookin. Always done it like that. First few years, Mum'd pester me to open em up in front of everyone, but longer it went on, I just sort of got left to it in the end.

Becky's got some bricks and a teddy bear, and her very first doll. As big as her, it is. Lovely seein her so happy. Fuckin lovely.

I'm watchin Becky open her last few things when I see Dad go behind the settee. And he pulls out this bike. This red fuckin Raleigh Chopper. Wheels it round to the middle of the front room, and I'm fuckin speechless. Dunno what to say, and I can feel the tears comin up again. Dad took me old bike down the dump ages ago when he cleared the garden out. Rusted to fuck, it was. Too small and rusted to fuck. Never thought I'd get another one. Fuckin never.

***

Me two aunts clubbed together and got me one of them roarin machines. You know the sort, stick em on your bike and they make it sound like a dragster. Everyone's got em. And Grandad's built a doll's house for Becky out of wood. Roof comes off, front comes open, bits of furniture, everything.

Clever old bastard, my grandad. Was our last Christmas with him. Keeled over Boxing Day right before Guns of Navarone. Fuckin hated that film, he did. Just couldn't bear to sit through it one more fuckin time, I reckon. Nan passed a few months later, and Dad weren't never the same after that. It's like he had his whole fuckin heart ripped out. But Christmas Day, with all of us there, Mum, Dad, Becky, me two aunties and Uncle Derek, Nan and Grandad, that was the best Christmas ever.

***

After we have our bacon sarnies, I pull up the curtains, see if it's snowin. Probably ain't even half-five yet. Pitch black outside, it is, but the street lamps are lightin up the whole world. And it ain't snowin, but it is rainin a bit, that soft sort of rain what seems to float down out the sky. Kenny ain't got no curtains up but his light's the only one on, so I see him straight off. I know he ain't seein me cos he's lookin right into the light of the street lamp outside his window. And he's got such a smile on his face. Such a fuckin smile.

Dunno why, but it's breakin me heart seein him like that. Breakin my fuckin heart. Mum tells me to shut the curtains cos it's lettin the cold in. Dad asks me if it's snowin. I tell him it's rainin and let the curtains drop back.

Can't believe I got a new bike, an that. Can't believe it. But I tell you what, after seein the way Kenny's smilin into that street lamp, that big, stupid grin all over his face, and that look in his eyes, I swear I'd swap everything I got for just one look at what he's seein in there.

***

They buried Grandad on the Wednesday before we went back to school. Mum sorted out Mrs Jessup next door to look after me and Becky while her and Dad was at the crematorium. She smells of cabbage, Mrs Jessup, and she's about three hundred years old. Always a bag of cough candy on the go. Mad as a box of fuckin frogs. Mum asks me if I want to see Grandad off, but I says no. Didn't see the point.

So, I'm upstairs helpin Becky with a bit of colourin, when the doorbell goes. I peek round the top of the bannisters to see who it is, but I can't see nothing cos Mrs Jessup's standin in the way. But I hear her all right.

'Come in, dear,' she says, sort of shaky, but all kind and sort of like my nan used to talk when one of us fell over and cut our knee or something. 'You'll catch your death out there,' she says.

She opens the door wider and moves to one side.

And there's Kenny. Standin in the rain, sort of starin blank, soaked to the fuckin skin, blood comin out the side of his mouth.

CHAPTER SIX

It's like Kenny don't even fuckin hear. So Mrs Jessup grabs him by the hand and sort of drags him in. That's when I come down the stairs, actin like I ain't seen nothing. It's only when Kenny stumbles into the hall, I see he ain't got nothing on his feet.

I watch as Mrs Jessup sort of guides him in the front room and plonks him on the settee. And he's lookin at me. Straight at me. Ain't natural, the look he's got on his face. Even when Mrs Jessup drags him past me, he ain't takin his eyes off me, like he's tryin to tell me something but he ain't got the words.

I go in the front room after I shut the front door, but Mrs Jessup sends me straight upstairs for a towel. The old girl might be mad, well, I mean, there ain't no fuckin argument about that, but she's all right, you know. I run up the stairs three at a time and jump off five on the way down. Nearly break me bleedin neck. I give Mrs Jessup the towel and she dries Kenny's hair a bit, then she wraps it round his shoulders and gets this old tissue out her pocket and dabs the blood off his mouth. Kenny don't even wince.

'You'll be all right, dear,' she says to him. 'You'll be all right.'

She ain't got no fuckin idea what this is all about. Fuckin none. Gives him a little pat on the head, then goes in the kitchen. Sort of puts me in mind of Miss Felton, people like that. They mean well, but they don't wanna get too fuckin close, you know.

Mrs Jessup comes out the kitchen couple minutes later with a plate of biscuits. No way Kenny's knockin them back, no matter what fuckin state he's in, and he grabs two handfuls. Becky comes down and she's behind the settee playin with her doll. She's too young to notice anything goin on. Fuckin good job an all. Ain't right havin littl'uns seein shit like this.

I ask Kenny what happened.

He's nibblin a Rich Tea and don't answer. Just keeps on fuckin nibblin. Shakin, he is, and it ain't just cos he's got nothing on his feet. I grab him round the shoulders.

'Kenny, mate,' I says. 'Look at me.'

It's like he still can't hear nothing. So I start shoutin at him.

He lifts his head up. Stops nibblin. White as a fuckin sheet. Can only be one thing put him in a state like this. It's all in what he does with his eyes. He looks at me, full on. Then he shuts em slow. It's like they don't shut, more sort of close over. Like a light goin out.

That's when I know his mum's in trouble.

Mum and Dad weren't gonna be back for ages, and Mrs Jessup, she weren't gonna be no fuckin use.

I check round the settee, see if Becky's all right, and leg it out the front door . . . SMASH.

Straight into me Uncle Derek. Big old bastard, me Uncle Derek. Six and a half foot. Built like a fuckin brick shit-house.

'Oi, oi, son,' he says, pickin me off the street. 'Where you off to?'

Weren't expectin to bump into him, but I'm fuckin glad I did. Hard bastard. Twenty years on the docks before they shut em down. Done a bit of bare knuckle in his time an all. I tell him about Kenny and Kenny's old man, and he tells me to go back inside and look after Kenny while he sorts out the old man.

But Kenny was always gonna be all right. We had a whole cupboard full of biscuits.

The heavens open up again. Can't hardly see for the rain pissin down. Uncle Derek pulls up his collar and goes over to Kenny's. And I got this idea to follow him. Dunno why. Sort of wanna make a difference, you know, for Kenny. Couple of steps and I'm soaked to the skin. Gotta go a bit slow so Uncle Derek don't see me, then I speed up when he gets in the house.

Front door's wide open. Uncle Derek's bent over Kenny's mum all twisted up at the bottom of the stairs. There's blood all over her face and her leg's fucked, all twisted up under her. She's breathin, though, so that's one thing. Uncle Derek's talkin to her close, right soft. Heart of gold, me Uncle Derek. You don't mess with that fucker, like I says, but heart of fuckin gold.

Uncle Derek hears me come in, but he don't turn round.

'Reckons she fell down the stairs,' he says. 'She said they ain't got a phone. Go back over and give the hospital a bell, son.'

Fell down the stairs? My fuckin arse. No way she fell down the fuckin stairs.

Can't see the old man nowhere. Then I hear this noise come out the front room. Uncle Derek's back talkin to Kenny's mum. Got his head right close to her, so he ain't heard nothing. I sneak me head round to where the noise is comin from.

And there he is. Fuckin bastard. Sittin there in his shitty armchair cryin his fuckin eyes out. Just like the last time I see him. Cunt.

Mum's voice comes out the hallway. Fuck. Must've come back to see where Uncle Derek's got to. And she's doin her fuckin pieces. Turns out my mum and Kenny's mum had got pretty close, you know. Women and all that. I go out in the hall. Mum's fuckin fumin. Her eyes is all big and swelled up and she's gone sort of purple.

'Where is he, Sandra? Where is that cunt?'

Ain't never heard me mum swear before, or since. Fuckin terrifyin. Then she clocks me.

'John, what are you –? Get back over and phone an ambulance. And hurry yourself about it.'

Loud sobbin from the front room, and Mum steams in there. Me and Uncle Derek look at each other. Then SLAP. I go in and the horrible bastard's on the floor coverin his head with his hands, screamin like a baby, and Mum's leanin over him, beatin the shit out of him with one of her shoes.

Uncle Derek shouts at me to get the ambulance, so I leg it back over home. After I've phoned em, I go in the front room to check on Kenny.

Kenny's watchin cartoons.

'She's all right, Kenny,' I says. 'She's all right.' I tell him the ambulance won't be long.

He looks round at me for a couple of seconds then sticks another biscuit in his gob.

I go and sit next to him.

Without takin his eyes off the telly, he tells me she fell down the stairs, and gets himself another biscuit.

I'm lookin out the window when the ambulance turns up. Mum's talkin to Kenny's old girl as they put her in the back, and she goes with her to the hospital. Uncle Derek's gone back in Kenny's, shuttin the door behind him.

***

When Mum comes back she does us some tea. What with Grandad bein a regular down the boozer, Tony the Governor's layin on a big old fuckin spread, so Dad was gonna be there ages yet. Uncle Derek's knuckles are all cracked open and I can't help starin at em as he's bitin into his cheese sarnie.

Mum's got it all sorted.

She says for me and Uncle Derek to go over Kenny's after tea to get Kenny's things so he can stay over ours till his mum gets out the hospital. Kenny don't leave off watchin telly while we're havin tea, won't even get off the settee, so he don't hear none of this. When I tell him what we're doin, he sort of jumps up really quick, like he can't wait to get over there.

Uncle Derek's got hold of a key and lets himself in Kenny's gaff like he's lived there his whole fuckin life. Kenny's run straight upstairs. I follow Uncle Derek in the front room soon as we get through the door. Kenny's bastard of an old man's sprawled out on the carpet. Ain't dead or nothing, I mean, he's just lifted his head up and he's lookin straight at me, so he can't be. But he's in a right fuckin mess. Holdin his ribs, blood smeared all over his face, and crusted up round his nose and ears. Breathin's fucked an all. Sounds like he's got his lungs in a fuckin vice. Like I said, you don't mess with me Uncle Derek.

And Kenny's old man's givin me this look like he's so sorry. Sort of pleadin. Throws me for a bit. But then I realise he thinks I'm Kenny. Can't see proper through the blood in his eyes, I reckon. Tries to spread his arms out to me but it hurts him too fuckin much, what with his ribs, and he starts cryin. Uncle Derek stays with him, sits on the seat by the door like a fuckin jailer, and tells me to go after Kenny.

When I get to Kenny's room, he's sittin on his bed, this scruffy little book in his hand. It's like one of them exercise books from school, other than Kenny's is yellow and ours are blue. Lookin at his face, I can see he ain't gonna be no fuckin use. So I start fillin the carrier bags Mum's give us. Turns out I only need a couple. Poor bastard's got fuck all. And the smell of piss, fuck, I just wanna get this done and get out of here quick as I fuckin can.

Mum empties the bags out when we get back over home. Nearly breaks her heart, lookin at her. Couple of school shirts, trousers, that flowery fuckin tie of his, and some shoes. All school stuff. That and about five grey socks and four ropey lookin pairs of pants. Nothing else at all.

Funny, I been sat next to Kenny all year and I never see how shit his stuff really was. The couple of shirts he's got is all odd buttons and grime stains, and the trousers are too short even for me, and I'm a couple inches shorter than Kenny. The tie's shit, fallin to pieces. As for the pants and socks, Mum chucks em straight in the bin. She turns the shirt collars inside out, and shakes her head, really sad. I sneak a look at what she was lookin at afterwards. Some other kids' names in em. Poor bastard. And the trousers. Second-hand shit. Fuckin all of it.

As for toys, there ain't none. Just that tatty yellow book. Kenny brought that over himself. Wouldn't let me touch it. Uncle Derek gets Kenny's bed over, and puts it in mine and Becky's room and moves Becky in with Mum and Dad.

***

I'm sittin on me bed first night Kenny stays with us, lookin at him scribblin in his book. And as I'm wonderin what's goin through his head and what he's writin, what the fuck he must be thinkin, he gets up and turns the light out. Not a fuckin word, just up and turns em out and sits back on his bed.

And that's how he stays. Just sittin. I know he's awake cos I see his outline and his eyes wide in the dark. And he's sittin with his legs crossed.

Starin at me.

CHAPTER SEVEN

Mum and Dad ain't flush or nothing, not by a long fuckin way, but it weren't like we was brassic neither. Every now and then Mum gets in a load of ironin or does a bit of cleanin, and Dad stays late at the factory, so either way, if they was a bit short Becks and me, we never feel it, just hear em shoutin about it sometimes. So when Kenny moves in, first thing Mum does is take him out and get him a load of new clothes.

And when they come home, Kenny's loaded up with bags of stuff. Pants, socks, shirts and trousers for school, and new shoes – turns out his other ones got cardboard stuffed down inside to cover the holes and Mum chucks em out. Then there's T-shirts, jeans, trainers. And he's got himself a new tie, not the ones with the elastic round neither. A proper fuckin tie. All of it up the cheap end, mind. All of it. Off the market mostly, but for Kenny, had to be like winnin the fuckin football pools.

After Mum's sent Kenny upstairs to try his new clobber on, she asks where Dad's gone. He's down the boozer with Uncle Derek, and when I tell her she ain't best pleased. Shakes her head and tightens her mouth, then goes in the kitchen and puts the kettle on.

A while later, Kenny comes down with his new gear on. And, blimey, you'd have thought he was off to see the fuckin Queen or something. Shirt tucked in, tie all done proper, shoes shiny as fuck. But he ain't sayin nothing. Not even a fuckin grin. I look at Mum and she's got a tear comin down her cheek. But she don't see Kenny like I do. She don't know the bleedin half of it. All she see is a boy in new clothes. And like I says, that ain't the half of it. Not with Kenny.

We go to bed early that night. Eight o'clock. First day back at school next day, and I can't wait. Love school, me. Not the lessons, they don't mean nothing, but knockin a tennis ball about in the playground with me mates, I could do that rest of me fuckin life. Mum has to take the pins out her mouth to kiss me goodnight. She's got all Kenny's clothes piled round her, sewin in name tags, and stuff. She don't kiss Kenny. She knows he ain't the sort.

And Dad still ain't home.

***

I hear the airin cupboard door go about midnight. That's where Mum keeps the spare blankets. Dad's on the settee again, then. Don't happen much, but after Grandad passed Dad's started drinkin loads, and Mum's proper fed up with it. Feel sorry for Dad. Feel sorry for em both. It's like they're losin each other and they don't even know it, just pushin each other away. Breaks me heart to see it. Can't say nothing, though. Dad's never in no state and Mum just shouts. Glad to be goin back to school, tell the truth, cos it's a fuckin nightmare round here.

***

Couple days at school and Wilkins is back after Kenny. I'm playin football with the lads in the playground at the time. Kenny ain't far off. Up against the railings, he is, watchin the cars go by. That's where he always stands. Whole playtime, sometimes. Out the corner of me eye, I see Wilkins go in Kenny's direction. Couple of the other lads see it an all, and we stop playin. I go over.

'Hello, Fatty,' Wilkins says. 'Have a good Christmas?' Kenny don't turn round. Just keeps watchin cars.

'Hear you got a new mum and dad.'

Little shit. Kenny turns round slow, and Wilkins starts takin the piss out of Kenny's new tie.

'Very nice. All wrapped up in a bit of newspaper, was it? Open it all by your fuckin self, did you? Lovely. Well done.'

Kenny's lookin at Wilkins, starin at him with those blank eyes of his. And he ain't sayin a word. I can tell Wilkins is shittin himself. Kenny's twice the size of the little fucker. Could lay him out in one hit, if he had a mind. But he don't. He just stares. Like I says, it's really shittin Wilkins up. Tell the truth, don't do much for me neither, so I step in. Tell him to fuck off.

Wilkins spins round.

'Fuck off yourself, Sissons. Just talkin to your little boyfriend here, that's all.'

I bang him in the face hard and he goes down like a sack of shit. Weedy little fucker. Blood's pissin out his nose and it looks like he's out cold for a second. Straight after, Kenny's back watchin cars and Wilkins crawls off to grass me up. Week's detention. Worth every fuckin minute.

***

Mum helps Kenny every night with his homework and does a bit of readin with him before bed, you know, help him along. And he's doin a bit better at school cos of it. Not much, I mean, even Mum must've got the idea by now Kenny ain't right in the head, but she's well chuffed when he's got a new word right, and stuff. Don't seem to make no difference to Kenny, though. Not as you could tell, anyway.

And you just can't keep him off the biscuits. Must've thought he'd fell into a fuckin biscuit barrel when he moved round our gaff. Fuckin gettin bigger and bigger, he is. Fuckin huge. And what with Mum's massive dinners, he ain't likely to get no fuckin smaller neither.

Wilkins never goes much near Kenny after I sorted him out, but I still kept me eye out for him, the little bastard. And then Jimmy Lawson starts goin mental. Losin the fuckin plot, he is. See him bangin his head against the school wall so hard once, cuts himself right open. Then he goes and tells Miss Felton he fell over. Natterin away to himself all the fuckin time an all, he is. I steer well fuckin clear of him. I tell Kenny to do the same.

***

So, I'm thinkin things is gettin better, but I know, deep down, Kenny ain't happy. He ain't happy at all. Never says a word to me, he don't. Not one fuckin word. Nod's about as much as I get out of him. Goin to school, comin home, in class – fuck all. Even at home, he never wants to play with me or nothing. It's not like he's horrible an that, it's more like he sort of don't even know I'm there. In his own little world, he is.

And he don't ever wanna go football with me and Dad on a Saturday neither. Dad does his best, but all Kenny wants to do is sit on his arse and watch cartoons. Mind you, the Hammers are doin fuckin rubbish this year, so I don't fuckin blame him.

Kenny's always much better with Mum than with Dad or me. She fusses round him like anything and when she's about, he sort of softens up. Colour comes in his cheeks, you know. She goes up with him on the train to the hospital most nights, see his old girl. And when he comes back, he goes straight to bed. Lies there with his eyes open or scribblin away in his little yellow book. If he ever cries, he does it bloody quiet, cos he never makes a sound. And his eyes always look the same anyway, so you can't tell nothing from that.

***

Kenny's still with us come Easter. Near on four months. And guess what? It's fuckin snowin. Dad builds a snowman out the front of the house. Put his Hammers scarf round it and one of me Grandad's old pipes in its mouth. Becky loves it. For the couple of weeks the snow's about, Dad takes the scarf off the snowman Fridays so's Mum can dry it for him to wear at the football Saturday. Then soon as he gets home, even before he comes in the door, he wraps that scarf back round the snowman's neck. Says it'll keep him warm. Silly sod.

So everything's lookin up. Loads of snow, and chocolate just round the corner. And the Hammers, bloody hell, we've just got through to the Cup Winners' Cup Final, like we did in sixty-five. We got Anderlecht this time. Come from Belgium, Dad says. He's talkin about me and him goin over on the ferry to see the game, but I know by the look in his eyes it's just the dreamin part of him sayin the words. Just like it always is.

Easter Sunday, we're all us kids in the front room. Dad's sittin in his chair readin the paper. Becky wants Swap Shop on the telly, but I can't stand it. Fuckin hate Noel Edmonds. We all do. Even Mum. Dad goes out the room cos he can't even stand to look at the cunt. Then Mum comes in.

'Kids?' she says, and we all look round.

Easter eggs. Three of em. One each for me, Becks, and Kenny. First one Kenny ever got, I reckon, seein his face when Mum's give it to him. Nearly fuckin falls over, he does.

So, me and Becks, we're layin on the floor in front of the telly, start breakin into our eggs straight away, like you're supposed to. After a minute, I'm wonderin why I ain't hearin no munchin behind me, I mean, fuck me, it's a chocolate egg, and it's Kenny, but I don't hear nothing. I look round, and he ain't even unwrapped it yet. Lookin at it, he is. Bloody lookin at it like it's made of fuckin gold or somethin. I mean, it is made of gold, the wrappin, you know, but it ain't fuckin *gold* gold.

'Go on, Kenny,' I says. 'It's only chocolate, mate.'

But he just sits there, starin at it.

Me and Becky do ours in no fuckin time. Faces covered in chocolate. Mum sits next to Kenny and says to him he can put it in the fridge if he likes, have it later. But he don't wanna let go of it and says he's takin it upstairs. He don't ask, just sort of tells her. That's Kenny all over, that is. You think he's the quietest, shyest kid in the world, but really, he does whatever the fuck he wants.

We swap comics and sweets what me dad brings home on a

Friday, and stuff, but that's about it. And all this time, the one thing I wanna find out is what he's writing in that bloody book. But he keeps it with him all the time. Don't let it out of his fuckin sight.

Like I says, Kenny don't have nothing to do with me, but Becky, Becky fuckin loves him. He plays with her for hours, he does. Runs her little wooden train round for her, sets up her bricks, makes her doll make funny noises, reads her books to her – about his level, to be honest. And he'll do anything to get a laugh out of her. Tickles her till you think she's gonna burst. Holds her up by her ankles and swings her about till she's gonna fuckin die laughin. He's fuckin great with her. Soon as we get home from school, even before we've had our biscuits, she's jumpin all over him. 'Ken Ken! Ken Ken! Pway bwiks, Ken Ken!' she says, and she runs up to him and he picks her up and they giggle and laugh like a pair of fuckin two year olds. Soon as I come along, his face turns to fuckin stone. Can't bleedin work it out for the fuckin life of me.

She's gonna be three in May, Becky, and Kenny, he's near on eight year older. Thought there was something wrong with him at first. You know, sort of mental, like. I mean, he's slow, Kenny, not right in the head, but there ain't nothing wrong with him in that way, you know, the way he plays with her. Just wants to make her happy. That's all.

I hear Dad say to Mum one night he don't think Kenny's mum's comin home. Him and Mum talk about it loads. Ain't like Dad's tryin to get rid of Kenny or nothing, just think, you know, he wants things back the way they was. Think we all do, really.

Don't hear fuck all from Kenny's old man. Ain't fuckin right. His own fuckin boy. We ain't got no reason to go over, but he ain't even bothered to knock see how Kenny's doin. Fuck him. That's what I reckon. Bloody fuck him. But Kenny's lookin out our front window at his old house all the fuckin time now, mumblin and twistin his hands together till his fingers go white. It's like he's really tore up inside, you know, really fuckin hurtin. He's changin. I can feel it.

I can feel it and it's scarin the fuckin shit out of me.

And fuckin Anderlecht, they beat us four-two in the final. Dad's ripped to bits over it. The situation with Kenny's been getting to us all, but us losin in the final like that, it's like it's pushed Dad closer to the edge than all of us.

And I got this feelin inside things is only gonna get fuckin worse.

CHAPTER EIGHT

When the end of the school year comes, it's bye, bye Bethnal Green Juniors. Mum and Miss Felton make it all up to be this big thing, like it's massive, or something. But it ain't. Truth is, I'm glad to leave the fuckin place. Come September we're all gonna be startin at Isaac Meade's anyway, just down the road, so it ain't like no one's never gonna see each other again. Not that I fuckin care. Some of the girls was in bits, though, but that's girls for you, ain't it. Goin round with their little books, gettin em signed by people they're gonna be seein in two months anyway. I didn't sign no ones. Told em all to fuck off. I got more important things on me mind, see, what with Kenny losin it and Dad and his drinkin.

He's still on a downer, Dad, since we lost to Anderlecht. He seemed to be doin all right with Grandad goin, but losin the final's sort of tipped him over, like he's only just realised Grandad's gone. He don't stop cryin and he don't stop drinkin. Mum does her best to bring it out of him, cheer him up, you know. Keeps tellin me and Becky he'll be all right soon. Think she's probably tellin herself that, an all. He never goes out, if he can help it, other than work and football. And me nan, Dad's mum, she ain't well neither. Grandad dyin like he did, sudden like, she died right with him. That's what I reckon. One night, Auntie Ivy pops round from the hospital and tells Dad the score. He puts his face in his hands and stays like that for fuckin ages.

Funny, when you're a kid you don't see your nan and grandad as nothing other than Nan and Grandad. It don't hit you it's your mum's mum or your dad's dad. And they're so old, you think they're gonna live for fuckin ever, you know. So when Nan went it hit me hard, really hard, cos they was both gone then. Mind you, broke Dad in two. Was like something went right out of him. Was only when I see him like that, I caught on there's some things you don't never get over.

Nan goin done Kenny in as much as the rest of us. When I say done him in, I mean it made him even worse than he was, you know. Set him back another fuckin hundred years. Weren't like he ever fuckin knew her. He just sort of joined in with the rest of us bein sad. Stopped playin with Becky, and everything. Bless her, she'd run up to him, but it's like he don't even see her. Walks straight past. Ends up me playin with her and I ain't half as good as Kenny with it. Couple of minutes. That's my hoppin pot.

I reckon he's like it cos he's missin his old girl. I told Mum but she just says he's been through a lot and we gotta be there for him. Says it sort of ratty, like she's up to here with it all. Me, Dad, Kenny, fuckin everyone. Specially Dad. She's got her right hands full with him, so I can see where she's comin from.

***

Middle of the school holidays, me and Kenny's on the floor in the front room playin 'Crossfire'. Dad bought it home from the market when he was on one of his good days. And when he come in with it, it was like he was gettin back to his old self again, but by the evenin he's sittin in his chair starin at the telly and puttin away cans of Skol like it's the last drop of drink on the fuckin planet.

Crossfire's great. Murder on your hand, though. Can only ever do ten minutes before me fingers come up all red and blisters. It don't hurt Kenny, though. And he's fuckin slaughterin me.

I let go of me gun, and shake me hand to get it workin again. Can't play no more cos me finger's all blistered up. But Kenny ain't takin no notice, just keeps on firin down at me. The metal ball thing's in my goal, where he shot it last, so he ain't got nothing to aim at, just keeps on crackin em out.

'Kenny!' I shout, cos I'm a bit pissed off now what with him takin no fuckin notice.

And he lifts his head up slow and looks at me in that blank way of his that's sort of scary till you got used to it. Even then it still puts the fuckin shivers up me.

I tell him loud and fuckin clear I ain't playin no more cos me finger's fucked. Too loud and fuckin clear, as it happens. Forgot Mum was in the kitchen.

'One more word like that, young man, and you'll be up them stairs before your feet touch the floor.'

Means it an all, she does. I tell her I'm sorry. Don't want no more grief, what with me finger killin me an all.

Kenny's lookin at me straight in the eye now, and he's firin them marbles a million miles an hour.

CRACK. CRACK. CRACK. CRACK.

He ain't even lookin where they're goin cos he ain't takin his eyes off me. And when he runs out, he carries on firin anyway. That's when I know he's on the fuckin way out.

Phone rings. Mum comes out the kitchen and answers. Uncle Derek's dragged me dad down the boozer, not that he needed much askin, so he ain't around. I go in the kitchen to make meself a jam sarnie. Kenny's still on the Crossfire. Not that I think he's playin by any fuckin stretch.

'Sandra, love, you okay?'

Fuck. Kenny's Mum. I never heard her phone here before.

I poke me head round in the hall where the phone is so as I can hear better. And Mum, Mum's got a face on her like a smacked arse. She's got her hand over her mouth and tears in her eyes. The old girl's comin home. Wants to make a go of it with the old man. Mum reckons it's a wrong un, obviously.

And me? I don't fuckin know. Geezer beats the shit out of a woman, puts her in the hospital, and she wants to 'make a go of it'

Take fuckin Einstein to work that one out.

Mum puts the phone down and I jump back in the kitchen, pretend I been here all the time. But Mum don't come in. She goes straight upstairs.

Next mornin, Kenny don't say nothing, even though I heard Mum tell him his old girl's movin back in a couple of days. And Mum, bein Mum, she wants to give the house a good clean out. Dad's back at work after Nan's passin, so Mum bells Auntie Ivy and Auntie Gwen. They both turn up wearin head scarves and aprons, and carryin buckets full of cleanin stuff.

Kenny shakes his head when Mum asks him if he wants to go over, so she leaves him to look after Becky. My job's sortin out Kenny's old room. Make it nice for him, you know. Mum don't know he ain't got no carpet and the floorboards smell of piss. I tell her I'll do me best. She gets the key off the top of the fridge and we all go over. Ninety fuckin degrees outside. Like wakin up in a fuckin oven. I look back home as I'm crossin. And Kenny's watchin me every step.

So we're comin up the front path. Mum's in front, then Auntie Gwen and Auntie Ivy, then me, but I smell it first. At least I'm the first one to say something. Suppose the others reckoned it was just the smell of the house, you know, bein a shit-hole and all that. But I know it weren't. Mum opens the door and steps back coughin with the smell.

And there he is. Kenny's old man. Hangin from the bannisters.

There's flies fuckin everywhere. Thousands of the fuckers. And the smell. Fuck, the smell. Like bein hit in the face with a fuckin shovel. Auntie Gwen screams something stupid like, 'Oh my gawd, the fucker's only gone and topped hisself!' and Auntie Ivy drops her bucket and staggers back in the street.

Mum gathers herself a bit and slams the door shut, holdin her hand over her mouth. I don't really see much. Enough to chuck me guts up in Auntie Gwen's bucket, mind.

Coppers reckoned he'd been hangin there about a week.

I'm wipin the sick off me chin when I see Kenny's still watchin from across the road. Becky's lookin at me funny, same way as when she wants me to play. Sort of a cross between please and help. Something's wrong. I know that. And it ain't Kenny's old man upsettin her. It's Kenny. He must've heard me Auntie Gwen shoutin out, but there ain't nothing on his face. Fuck all. Don't even come over. Just stands there, holdin Becky's hand.

I'm lookin at Kenny then at Becky. And she's cryin. Not loud, but there's these little tears comin down her face. Mum and Auntie Gwen and Auntie Ivy are natterin ten to the fuckin dozen behind me and don't see nothing. Becky tries to pull her hand out but Kenny's squeezin it so hard she can't get away. Then she screams.

I leg it cross the road, and the whole world's roarin in me ears. Soon as I gets there, Mum and me aunties come up behind. Kenny lets go of Becky's hand and she runs behind me and grabs onto me legs. Mum says, 'Kenny, love,' real soft and gentle, and the poor fucker keels right over into her arms.

CHAPTER NINE

Kenny and his mum stay at our gaff while the Old Bill move in. The Council shut down the house after and take the boards off the one next door. Said they'd clean it out and Kenny and his old girl can move in when they like. His old girl's cryin all the time. Mum spends most days with her arms round her. Kenny don't say nothing. Not to no one. Then one day, he opens up, starts talkin. Not about his old man, nothing like that, just about the weather or what's on telly. Boring shit. Fuckin weird. But he don't wanna go out the house. Our house. Not ever. Says it's too hot, like he's gonna melt or something. Really means it an all.

I try and push him a couple times, you know, really encourage him, like. But that look comes back on his face, the one I saw him give Wilkins in the playground that time, and what he give me when we was playin Crossfire. I back straight off. Then he's smilin again, askin me if he can look at me Beano. I keep him away from Becky, not that he's got much interest in her anymore. Shuts himself up in the bedroom, comes down for something to eat, then he's straight back upstairs again.

It's a couple of weeks by the time the Council sort Kenny and his mum's new place out. We all goes over when it's done. New doors, everything painted up, curtains, the fuckin lot. Like a new fuckin house, it is. And Kenny's got a proper room, like he always should've done. Like a new start for em both, you know – Kenny and his mum. That's what I reckon.

***

But his mum's round ours all the time. She reckons Kenny don't never come out his room. Locks himself away. And she looks fuckin awful, his mum. Like she's aged forty years.

By the end of the summer, Kenny's curtains are gone and his carpet's dumped out front. Only time I ever see him is when he's lookin out his bedroom window. He's there all the time, like he's lookin for something that ain't there no more. But when that street light comes on outside his window, he don't take his fuckin eyes off it.

School holidays done, and it's first day at Isaac Meade. It's three times the size of Bethnal Green Juniors. Fuckin massive, it is. Soon as we get in, we all get sent down the hall. There's fuckin hundreds of us, waitin to be put in classes. The teachers are standin all round, and you can tell there ain't no Miss Feltons here. You can see it in their eyes.

Out front's the Headmaster. Skinny, evil, fucker. Tweed suit. Little pointy beard. Eyes like a fuckin snake. His name's Mr Jackson. Reminds me of Kenny's old man.

We all get called in the end, and me and Kenny's in the same class. Mr Brandon. '1B' – class full of morons, thickos, gommos, and fuck-wits. Bottom of the bleedin barrel. That's us. Thommo's with us, though, so least it's gonna be a laugh.

Soon as we walk in, Kenny goes and sits right at the back in the corner, by the window. Before I can get there, some drippy fucker – glasses and greasy hair – goes and sits next to him. Thommo's pissin about down the corridor, and he ain't even come in yet, so I sit at an empty desk a few along from Kenny. And this black kid what I ain't never see before comes and sits next to me. After Brandon's quieted us all down, he gets us to talk to who's sat next to us for ten minutes, you know, one of them bollocks things so as we can get to know each other and tell the whole class about em. Then Brandon goes out. Fuckin leaves us to it, don't he. Pretty much all of us know each other anyways from Juniors, so most of the kids are just havin a laugh and fuckin about soon as we're left on our own.

Now I ain't got nothin against the blacks, you know, not like some. Me Grandad, he was fuckin terrible. Reckoned they should've all been sent back on fuckin banana boats. I'd say to him, 'What about Clyde Best?' but he reckons that was different. 'Clyde Best is an 'ammer, son,' he used to say. 'One of us.'

Everyone else is talkin and laughin and pissin about, like I says, other than Kenny and the drippy fucker next to him. They're just starin out the window, both of them, like they're waitin for a fuckin spaceship to land, or something. And I gotta talk to this black kid. He ain't even lookin at me, just lookin out front.

'All right?' I says.

He nods his head, slow. Can't even see his face proper. Thought he might turn round. But he don't. Fuck, this is gonna be hard.

'My name's John. Johnny Sissons.'

He spins round, his eyes big, dartin into me, like I've just kicked him in the stomach.

'Like from the Preston final in sixty-four?' he says.

Fuck me. First thing takes me back is he talks just like me, you know, like the way I talk. Dunno why, thought he'd be like one of them blokes off the Black and White Minstrels, you know, 'Mammy', and all that bollocks. But he ain't. He's just like me.

'That's right,' I says. 'Johnny Sissons, youngest player ever to score in a Cup Final.'

'And are you –?'

'No. Dad reckons he's some sort of cousin, or something, but I ain't never met him.'

And we don't stop talkin for fuckin ages.

When it is our turn to talk about each other to the class, we're fucked. All we been doin is talkin about the Hammers. Don't know fuck all about him, other than his name's Keith. Brandon gives us up for a lost cause. Shakes his head, breathes out deep, and moves on.

'You two, at the back, in the corner.'

Kenny. Nothing. Brandon raises his voice.

'I said, you two boys, in the corner. Tell me something. *Please,* tell me something.'

Sarcastic cunt.

Kenny's still lookin out the window. There ain't no touchin him when he's lost like this. The other kid next to him's whisperin that he don't know, but it's so quiet, only us near him can hear. Brandon comes over, sort of marchin, one of them big, long, wooden metre sticks in his hand. He weren't never gonna pick on me and Keith, Brandon. He see we got a bit of lip about us, but Kenny and this other kid, they're easy fuckin pickings for the likes of cunts like him. He slams the metre stick on drippy kid's desk. BANG. The kid's shakin, gone all red. Reckon he's gonna cry. Brandon leans right into him, speaks all quiet.

'What's his name?'

'I don't know, sir.' Quiet as you like.

'Speak up, boy. You want the class to hear you, don't you, boy?'

'Yes, sir.' Like a fuckin mouse.

Bang. Metre stick slams on the desk again.

'What is his name?'

'I don't know, sir.'

'You don't know? Why don't you know, boy? Are you stupid or something, boy? Is that it? Are you stupid?'

There's a few laughs. But I ain't one of them. Nor's Keith.

'Yes, sir.'

'Yes, sir, what, sir?

'Yes, sir. I'm stupid, sir.'

There's a few more laughs, but they're stopped when Brandon smashes the metre stick down on the desk again, and it catches the kids fingers. He screams. Starts cryin really soft.

'And you, looking out the window.' Shit. Kenny. 'See anything interesting, boy? Anything you'd like to tell the whole class about?' Brandon's got this smirk on his face now, like he's on a fuckin roll. Really enjoying himself, he is. Slams the metre stick on Kenny's desk. Kenny don't even jump, just turns round slow. The kid next to him's bawlin his eyes out, so only me and Brandon's close enough to see the empty look in Kenny's eyes. Kenny's starin at Brandon cold. Not a fuckin word. Shits Brandon right up. He weren't expectin that, and the metre stick's shakin in his hand.

This Brandon's a right bastard. One of them cowardly cunts, you know. The fuckin worst sort.

Brandon can't handle Kenny starin at him for more than a couple of seconds, and he's back up the front of the class before you fuckin know it.

'Open your form books and write one page about yourselves.'

Straight to the fuckin point.

And he's on his way out the door.

'I'll be back in a minute,' he says.

Probably goin to have a little snifter of somethin out the staff room. Some kid puts his hand up.

'Sir? I haven't got –.'

'JUST DO IT.'

Door slams. Gone.

Turns out Keith just moved in from Canning Town. And he's Hammers fuckin mad. Tall and lanky, he is. Just lookin at him, you can tell he's hard. Solid, you know. And he's got eyes like Lawson's, like there ain't nothing he won't do if he got a mind. But Keith's different to Lawson. He ain't fuckin mental, for a start. He's the most solidest bloke I ever met. It's like he's all sort of coiled up, waitin for something to happen. And when it does, when the time comes, he's gonna tear the whole fuckin world apart.

***

Was right about Jackson, the headmaster. A right cunt. Clouts you round the head for your shirt hangin out, and if he see you runnin in the corridor, cunt sticks his leg out sends you fuckin flyin. Talk back to him and he pulls your ear half off your head, sticks his face right close till you can taste his scummy breath and drags you in his office. Then he canes your arse off till you can't walk for a fuckin week. Never does no classes. It's like his job's to fuckin go round the school lookin for kids he can fuckin hurt. Cunt.

Weeks go by and Kenny keeps his head down, pretty much, and me and Keith and Thommo, we look out for him best we can. But I see Kenny when no one's lookin and he makes me fuckin nervous. I know it's comin. It's like something's buildin up inside him. Just sort of gazes, like he's somewhere else.

Picks his fingers all the time. Picks em till they bleed.

And it don't take a few months before it gets too fuckin rough for Kenny. I was all right. If you was half tasty kickin a tennis ball round, like I was, or funny, like Thommo or hard, like Keith, you was always gonna be all right. And if you was a fuckin swot, you was gonna be all right an all cos you can do other people's homework and stuff. You got a fuckin use, you know. Anywhere in between, you was fucked.

I keep out all that shit, me. Only thing I'm interested in is a kick-about playtimes and lunch. Like I said, though, Kenny, Kenny was fucked from the start. I mean, what's there not to pick on? He's fat, stupid, can't kick a ball to save his fuckin life, knows fuck all about football and stinks like a fuckin dustbin. And he fuckin takes it all. Everyone thinks he's a bit psycho, but he don't do nothing about it. Every fuckin kick and punch and head down the shit-house. Takes the fuckin lot.

Come to a head afternoon playtime one Thursday. I'm playin football at the top of the playground with Keith and all the regulars. Thommo's in with Mrs Henderson for chuckin a hairbrush at her in French. Kenny's at the bottom of the playground by the main doors, waitin to go back in. Me and David Watson's team captains, bein the best in our little lot. After I make sure Keith's on my team, I pick all the shit kids, you know, the real fuckin shit.

Love a game of football they do, but can't play for fuckin toffee. We lose every time we play, but scorin a goal, just one, that's like winnin the whole fuckin game itself. And in this one, our lot's playin out their fuckin skins. Well, no, me and Keith's playin out our fuckin skins. But they ain't doin bad, really tryin, you know.

There's only a few minutes left till the end of break and, some-fuckin-how, we're eleven-all. I got eight, Keith's got three. Keith passes to me and I stop it under me left foot. Only one thing on me mind. Stevie Mitchell's frontin me up, knowin there ain't long till the bell. Stevie's a big lad, and he's snarlin at me like a fuckin Rottweiler. Keith's screamin at me to pass back to him, but I'm fucked if I'm gonna do that. I'm Geoff Hurst, see, George Best, Johan fuckin Cruyff. I one-two it off the playground wall and sprint round Stevie Mitchell.

And Sissons is through, just two more to beat. He skins the first like he ain't there and passes out wide to Putsy Jenkins, the two foot midget with the dodgy teeth. But Putsy's pickin his nose. Shit. He's got no idea where he fuckin is. But just before he gets mullered by their fat second year ringer, Putsy takes a swing at the ball and sends it back across goal. Everyone stops and looks at him, wonderin how the fuck he's managed that, and here comes Sissons. His eye on the ball, his heart in his mouth . . . dives, full fuckin length, what a header, right past the keeper. Best goal this playground ever fuckin see.

I've pounded into the railings at the front of the school where the goal is, and all the shit kids have piled on top of me, dribblin and laughin and, fuck me, the smell's something fuckin awful.

As I'm pickin myself up, dustin meself off, I look up for Kenny and see him bein took away by a couple of older kids. Third year wankers. I've seen em about, and they're fuckin bad news.

At the back of the school, where they've took him, there's a way down to the caretaker's office in the basement. It's like a little fenced off corner of the playground with a gate to a load of metal steps goin down. When the caretaker leaves the gate open, kids get chucked down. Everyone calls it 'The Gobbin Chamber'. And that's where they're takin Kenny.

There's a crowd followin. I'm sprintin over. Keith's clocked it and he's followin me. We leg it round the back, but we're too late. There's like a fuckin bayin mob there already. Kids shoutin and tauntin all pressed right up to the railings. I squeeze myself through before Keith cos I'm littler than him. And I see Kenny walkin down the steps, like he's got all the time in the world. And the kids near the front, mostly third and fourth years are gobbin on him like he's a fuckin animal. When he gets to the bottom, he sits on the ground and tucks his knees up to his chin, and wraps his arms round em. Then it starts fuckin rainin gob and mud and snot like you wouldn't fuckin believe.

Some kid, some horrible little fucker, starts pissin through the railings and it's landin right on Kenny's back. I'm too crushed to take a swing at the cunt, so I get in his face and knee him in the bollocks. That starts a right fuckin free-for-all. And I'm swingin and kickin for all I'm fuckin worth. Keith's doin the same a little way off. He breaks through to me and we're back to back, fightin for Kenny. Well, I'm fightin for Kenny. Keith's just fightin. Course, we don't last long.

On the edge, just watchin, there's a couple of fifth years. Graham Allerton, hardest kid in the school, and next to him, this slimy, weedy little fucker. Terry Wilkins. Older brother to that horrible cunt, Harry Wilkins. Allerton and Terry Wilkins are just watchin us, me and Keith, gettin a right fuckin pastin.

I'm in as bad a state as Kenny at the end. Gob and blood all over me, face pressed up against the railings. I look down at him, at his face. In his eyes.

And there ain't nothing left.

CHAPTER TEN

Next day, we're in the school canteen havin lunch. I'm fucked off cos it's pissin down outside, so there's no chance of a kick-about. I'm lookin at the pile of shit what they dished up on me plate. Fuckin sausage, mash and peas. Sausage, mash and fuckin peas. Same shit every week, whether it's liver and onions or faggots or shepherd's pie or sausage, mash and fuckin peas. It's all shit.

Kenny's sittin next to me, Keith and Thommo opposite. Harry Wilkins is a couple of tables up, whisperin with them two third year fuckers what dragged Kenny down The Gobbin Chamber. He's latched onto em last couple of months. Harry Wilkins, back to his old weaslin ways.

A sausage comes flyin over, just misses Kenny, bounces off the table, and lands in the aisle.

I get on with me dinner. I ain't in the mood for this. Rain's really pissed me off. Feels like I'm all caged up, you know, and I just wanna get out.

'Go on, Fatty, bit extra for you, pick it up, there's a good boy.'

Wilkins. Cunt. Another sausage bounces off the table. Kenny's tensed up next to me, hands shakin, knife and fork rattlin on his plate. It's comin. I can feel it. Ain't no way back now. It's like the whole place has gone quiet but it ain't, just I can't hear nothing cos Kenny's cut the sound off.

Teachers are chattin up top and none of em notice Wilkins and his two mates comin over. Kenny don't move a fuckin inch. Wilkins leans in close. The slimy fucker's been waitin ages for this. Thinks cos he's got his mates with him, I won't step in.

'You gonna fuckin pick em up, Fatty?' Wilkins says, sort of sneerin. 'Or have I gotta fuckin make you?'

Everything's movin slow now, other than Kenny. He ain't movin at all. Wilkins has got a face on him like he owns the whole fuckin world, and I wanna slap him so hard he'll think he's been hit by a fuckin train. But this is Kenny's fight.

Keith's lookin at me, and I'm lookin at Thommo. It's like we're stuck in our seats, stuck in a moment, and best we can do is stay with it. And there still ain't no sound. I see Wilkins' mouth movin and I see his mates laughin and I see the teachers yackin, but I don't hear none of it.

Then . . . BANG.

Kenny's smacked Wilkins right in the face with the bottom of the fuckin dinner tray. It's like a spell's broke and the whole fuckin place goes mental. Tables goin over, food flyin all round the place, kids chuckin all sorts of shit. Mash, prunes, custard, sausages, peas. Teachers can't do fuck all.

Thommo's pissin himself and Keith's stood up, ready for whatever's comin – teachers, fourth years, fifth years, fuckin anyone. I'd be standin with him, but I'm tryin to drag Kenny off Wilkins. He's sittin on top of the cunt, batterin his face with the dinner tray so hard it's like he's gonna fuckin kill him. And he's roarin every time he smacks him. Like an animal. Wilkins is screamin like a tart and Kenny keeps on bangin that dinner tray straight into his face.

'Fuckin leave it, Kenny,' I shouts. 'Fuckin leave it.'

I'm thinkin he really is gonna fuckin kill the cunt, but there ain't nothing I can do about that. Ask me, I reckon he's got it comin. I'm lookin at Kenny, in his eyes, when he comes up for another smack and it's like he don't even know what the fuck he's doin or where he even fuckin is. Just keeps on bringin that tray down like he can't stop.

Mr Pugh the rugby teacher bundles through and has a go at draggin Kenny off. Big bloke, Pugh. Welsh. Told us first day football was for poofs. Fuckin wanker. But he ain't got no fuckin chance. Two other teachers jump in to help him out, and Wilkins squirms out from under Kenny, nose splattered right cross his face, lyin on the floor in a right fuckin state.

I tread on his bollocks as he's lying there. Thommo tips a plate of dinner on his face and Keith coughs up a greeny and flobs it on top.

Meanwhile, Kenny's in right fuckin lumber. They're draggin him out the canteen, Pugh and the others, arms up his back, head down like he's a fuckin serial killer.

***

School writ a letter home after the canteen fight. Mum was fuckin fumin. But when I tells her about Kenny, she just sits down. She don't say nothin. Dad don't even read the letter.

Kenny gets shifted out to some Borstal in Kent. Mum takes his old girl on the train to visit of a weekend. I go once, but Kenny's so monged out he don't even know who I am.

Fuckin cried all the way home, I did, sittin on that train, lookin out the window tryin to make sense of it all. Weren't like we was even mates, or nothing, me and Kenny. Not really. I mean, he hardly said a fuckin word to me all them years. But we shared a life. And that sort of means something to a kid, you know.

***

A few months later, Kenny's moved to some nutty kids' place in the sticks. Mum says it's for his own good. Reckon they can help him better out there.

No one to help his old girl, though. She's took a right turn for the worse. Poor fuckin cow. See her at night, at his bedroom window, tryin to put his curtains back up. Don't get halfway before she breaks down. Drops the whole fuckin lot and starts over. She's at it for fuckin hours sometimes.

And every now and then, she has a go at draggin Kenny's old carpet back in the house. Covered in shit and soaked right through it is. Can't even shift it one fuckin inch. Dad keeps sayin he wants to go over and help her out, put the curtains back up and sort out a new carpet, but Mum says to leave it. First thing that's brought Dad to life for fuckin ages, though, seein Kenny's old girl like that. He's right worried about her. But Mum says she was gonna be all right. Just take a bit of time is all. It's like Mum knows what's goin on in the old girl's head and won't have Dad interfering.

Dad tells me on the sly, he reckons Kenny's old girl needs lookin at, like she's goin off her rocker or something. I see him starin out the window sometimes, just like Kenny used to do and that's when I know it's rippin him to bloody pieces seein Kenny's old girl like that.

***

Things settle down pretty quick at school after Kenny goes. Wilkins is off for ages and when he comes back, he's a fuckin shell. Kenny really made his mark on that cunt. No fucker wants to know him, and he got chucked down The Gobbin Chamber twice in the first week – first time by his own fuckin brother. Ain't sayin he never had it comin, but I never went near when they threw him in. Couldn't look down that pit without thinkin of Kenny.

Terry Wilkins said to let him know if the little wanker's givin us any grief and he'll sort it out. But he ain't no fuckin better than his little brother. Two peas out the same fuckin pod, if you ask me. That's what I reckon.

Teachers got it right in for the rest of us all year. Can't even fart without em draggin you down to Jacko's office. Bit of a problem for Thommo, what with his performin arse. Jacko has a fuckin field day with him.

The weeks go by, and the months. I'm keepin me nose clean best I can. And before you know it, end of first year's come round. And the whole of the last term's about just one fuckin thing, ain't it. The Queen's fuckin Silver Jubilee wotsit bollocks. Load of fuckin shit.

They got us makin flags and banners and streamers, even writin letters. As if she's gonna open anything with a fuckin 'Bethnal Green' stamp on it. Me and Keith and Thommo writ we wanted to shit on her throne and eat her dogs. Can't think what Jimmy Lawson writ, the mad bastard.

Never knew neither. It's round this time he gets his cock out in maths and they cart him off to the same nut-house Kenny's banged up in. What are the fuckin chances of that, eh? Same fuckin nut-house.

Back home, Mum's helpin out with the street party stuff and tryin to get Dad off his arse to give her a hand. But Dad ain't havin none of it. Hates the Royal Family, Dad does, just like Grandad before him. Always made us stand up for the National Anthem, mind, when England was playin. But he reckons that was about supportin the lads, Queen's got fuck all to do with it.

Mum's more traditional. Buys all the shit. Jubilee tea-towels, stupid fuckin Union Jack hats, mug each for me and Becky.

Come the day, there's a load of street races outside, you know, egg and spoon, and shit, and a big old party. All right for the littl'uns, I suppose, but I'm gonna be thirteen in a few months. What do I want with all that shit? Mum makes me do the runnin race, though. Feel like a right bleedin idiot. Come second behind some eight-year-old with a fucked lip. Mum said I weren't even tryin. Fuckin right. Gives me a clip round the ear for me troubles and sends me inside to sit with Dad. He ain't comin out for nothing. No fuckin way.

Sittin in his armchair, he is, can of Skol in one hand and the Union Jack hat on his head what Mum's made him wear. Starts bangin on about how come the revolution all the bastards'll be up against the wall. Get rid of the fuckers in one hit, he says. Reckons the Russians had the right idea. Pissed already, he is. That's why Mum's stayin outside. She can't stand seein him like this no more. He's down the boozer most nights, my dad. Just so's he can get out the house, I reckon. Never really talks much at home and always got this look on his face like everything's too much. With Nan and Grandad gone, it's like he's turned into a little kid. Always sulkin. Him and Mum rowin all the time, when they can be bothered to say anything to each other at all.

Fuckin ain't the same no more.

Dad still watches the Hammers of a Saturday, mind, but even that ain't like it used to be. Used to be like he couldn't give a fuck about the result, other than the big matches. Always used to say, 'As long as the lads put a fuckin battle up, that'll do me'. Now it's like every match is fuckin life and death. If we lose, he don't talk to no one for fuckin days. Win, and he's over the fuckin moon twice over. But none of it's real, you know.

Becky's out in the street havin a blindin time. Little flag in her hand, wavin it mad as anything. Bless her. She still asks after her Kenny, you know. Really misses him. He's been gone about eight months come the Jubilee. I think about him all the time.

Street party ain't finished for hours yet. No way I'm goin out there again. Mum'd only drag me into another fuckin stupid race. So I'm stuck inside, and Dad's still bangin on about the fuckin revolution, sittin there in his Union Jack hat cos he's too scared to take it off. Mum's spent a load of dough we ain't got on shit and stuff for the fuckin Queen's fuckin Jubilee, and the Queen don't even fuckin know cos she's up at Buck-fuckin-House sippin tea with the rest of the fuckin inbreds. And I'm lookin at the flags outside, all them little flags, and all them people laughin and cheerin, and Kenny's old girl up at his window tryin to put his curtains up for the hundreth time, and I'm thinkin of Kenny, wonderin which one of us is in the real fuckin nut-house.

Jubilee dies a death soon as it's over. Couple of months after, I'm havin me tea when it comes on the radio Elvis is dead. Dad's at work, so least I don't see his face. Don't think I coulda stood that. When he comes in, he goes straight in his chair, holdin tight on the arms like it's the only safe place in the whole fuckin world.

CHAPTER ELEVEN

Dad's still wrecked over Elvis, so when he comes home one day, more pissed than normal, I don't think nothing of it.

We're havin our tea, me, Mum, and Becky, and when Dad comes in he's got his face all red and blotchy and he ain't walkin straight. Ain't even coverin up for Mum, which ain't a good fuckin sign. He throws his coat over the settee and leans on the back to stop from fallin over.

Mum's sittin at the table with her back to him. They ain't hardly said a word since they had a big barney after the Jubilee about his drinkin. And Becky's too busy tryin to stop Mum feedin her peas to notice Dad's even walked in the front door.

'Come on, Becky,' Mum says, 'just eat a few up, there's a good girl.'

Dad's squeezin his eyes with his thumb and finger like he's tryin to push all the tears back in.

'No want peas,' Becky says, and zips her mouth shut and folds her arms.

'Dad?' I says. 'You all right?'

Mum sees the look on me face and turns round. Me and her both know it's more than Elvis. Dad takes a deep breath and blows it out long and hard, and tells Mum the factory's gone to the wall. She gets up and goes over to him, and holds him tight.

What with Grandad, Nan, Elvis and now this, I dunno how much more Dad can take.

'Come and sit down, Bill.' It's the softest I've heard Mum speak to him in ages. 'I'll put the kettle on.'

And with that, Mum and Dad was speakin again.

Mum asks me to sort Becky out with her dinner, and her and Dad go and sits down on the settee. I sit in Mum's seat at the table so I can hear what they're sayin.

Becky's bein a pain in the arse. Won't eat nothing. Soon as I take me eyes off her, the little mare scarpers in the front room. Runs up to Dad and jumps on his lap and holds him tight like Mum. Just wants to make it all right for him. Whatever it is. Just wants to make it all right. Bless her.

Mum tells me to come and get Becky, but she's back before I've even got up.

'No peas, John John. No peas.'

I tell her to sit down, and she does it with this sort of end of the world look on her face. Then I do me big eyes at her and a big wide mouth, scoop up a big spoon of peas, and stick em right in me gob. Becks nearly falls off her chair with her gigglin. That's enough for me, though. Fuckin hate peas. I get up, quickly spit em in the bin and start clearin the table. Becky's holdin onto me legs and I'm draggin her cross the kitchen, clearin up quiet so as I can hear what Mum and Dad are sayin.

Some of them's been there thirty years and more, Dad says. He's done fifteen himself. Been there since before I was born. Never use to say much about what he did whenever I asked him. Sort of embarrassed, like he was ashamed or something. Mum'd always say something like, 'Your father? What does he do? As little as possible, son. That's what he does.' Then she'd laugh. She knew his job was shit – probably just puttin things in boxes or something – and she knew it made him feel less of a man in the doin of it. But it's how he provided for us, and that's what mattered to him more than anything. That's why he did those long hours in that shit-hole of a factory. That's what made him a man.

But all that's gone now.

Mum says she'll see if there's anything goin in the supermarket where Auntie Ivy works. But Dad's proper old school. Won't have Mum workin, won't have none of it. Won't sign on, neither. Proud, my dad. And the thought of Mum out at work sort of pulls him together a bit. Tells her not to worry, he'll pick something up.

Couple weeks later, he's queuein up at the Social like all the other poor bastards, and Mum's stackin shelves with Auntie Ivy at Fairways.

***

Always gonna take its toll on Dad, all the shit he's been through. And the drinkin just tops it off. Most mornings he don't even get up in time to see Mum off to work. Sparko in bed, he is. Fucked. I end up givin Auntie Gwen a bell so she can come round and look after Becky while I go to school.

Becky ain't gonna be startin playgroup for another year, and Auntie Gwen's said she'll help out lookin after her so Dad can go out lookin for a job. But it don't work like that. Most days she's still here come tea-time knockin us up something to eat.

Dad has his good days, though, and he'll go down the Job Centre, see what's there. Tells me it won't be long before he's back on his feet. But he don't have no luck. His luck run out a long fuckin time back.

I know Mum's been down the doctor's with him a couple of times, and he's on tablets cos I see him take em and Mum's always on at him to make sure he remembers. But they don't tell me nothing. Neither one of em. And he's started havin these moods, you know, like he's really fuckin nasty sometimes. Other times he won't say a word for days.

No matter how hard things get, Dad never misses a match up at the Boleyn. I'm in the school team now and I'll have a kick-about in the street or over The Barmy till the cows come home, but I ain't never been one too much for watchin. But I go with Dad every home game now. Keep him company. And I tell you what, standin on them terraces, with my dad, and thousands of others all singin, chantin, swearin and jokin, well, there ain't nothing fuckin like it. Sorta know now when Dad used to say it weren't never really about the score, you know. More about the bein there. Together. Good fuckin job it ain't about the score, cos we're doin really shit this season. I mean, really fuckin shit. We can all see where it's headin but neither fuckin one of us is sayin a word about it.

On a good day, when Dad's up for talkin an that, me and him go over the game on the way home, slag the ref off, read bits out the programme, try and work out why we lost. We always end up laughin goin in the front door. He puts his arm round me shoulder and says it ain't about the result, it's about the stickin together when it's all fallin down round your ears, knowin it's all gonna get a whole fuckin lot worse. And how we fuckin laugh.

Other times, when Dad's on a downer, we come back from football not sayin a fuckin word. He goes in and sits in his chair and I go up and lie on me bed lookin at the ceilin feelin like there's something missin.

Even though Dad's still outta work, and Mum brings home hardly nothing, she never stops him goin. It's like she knows it gives him more than she understands. Something he can make sense of, you know. Fuck knows there's nothing else.

It's got so bad we gotta beat Liverpool last game of the season to stay up, and not even Dad thinks we got a fuckin prayer with that one.

***

The Boleyn Ground 29th April Nineteen seventy-eight
Hammers 0-2 Liverpool

***

Mum and Becks is in bed, and me and Dad's in the front room sittin quiet in the dark, listenin to Elvis. We don't say nothing about the match. I mean, what's left to say? When it comes down to it, all the buzz and the stickin together and the singin, and all that bollocks, don't mean a fuck.

We been relegated to the Second Division for the first time in twenty years. Dad still ain't got a job, and Elvis?

Elvis ain't never comin back.

CHAPTER TWELVE

After Kenny went, Keith, me, and Thommo got right tight. Ain't like we weren't mates before or nothing, just I always had one eye out for Kenny, you know. They did an all, but mostly they done it cos of me. As for Kenny, ain't heard nothing in ages. Sometimes wonder what he's doin, if he's all right. That sort of thing. But life goes on, don't it? Becky talks about him sometimes. Asks me when the nice fat boy's comin back. I tell her I dunno, and every time I say it, the whole world goes black.

As for school, nothing to tell. See, when you're thick, like me, it's a piece of piss. No one expects nothing of you, and comes a time when you don't expect nothing of yourself. And the time fuckin flies by. Before I know it, end of fifth year's comin round and I'm nearly out. Can't fuckin wait. Not that I go much anyway, mind.

Mum's changed her hours cos Becky's at school now. Second year Infants. Think it's so she can keep an eye on me an all. Make sure I got to school, like. But most days, soon as I'm out the door, I'm straight round Thommo's gaff. His old man's out early hours on his stall, so the house is empty. Keith meets us there, and we change out of our school clobber and head up west on the train.

First stop's Hari's Paki shop round the corner from Thommo's. That's where we nick some sweets for the trip, and Keith picks us up some fags. He's the oldest lookin of us, see, so he can get away with it. Mind you, old Hari would sell his own fuckin mother if he thought he could make a few fuckin pennies on it.

Me and Keith's on half a pack of fags a day and I have to shove a tonne of Wrigleys down me throat to hide the smell from Mum. Thommo's into glue. Always got a bag on him. Never done nothing for me, if I'm honest. Just give me a fuckin headache.

We head for Soho first, more often than not, you know, just for laugh. Then it's up Oxford Street, Tottenham Court Road, round there. I nab a couple of tapes where I can; Stiff Little Fingers, The Clash, Ramones, that sort of thing. Thommo picks up whatever he can stuff up his snout for later, mostly marker pens and Tipp-Ex. Keith never nicks nothing. It's the bein outta school that's his buzz. The freedom. The walkin tall. That, and bein our fag man.

Ten years at school and none of us got fuck all to show. Nothing.

Not a fuckin sausage.

But Becky, she's just startin out. Like I said, second year Infants. And good luck to her, that's what I bleedin say. Mum's too busy with her to bother much with me. Fair enough, really. Mind you, she always makes sure I'm out the door for school on time, even when she knows I ain't goin. Watches me all the way down the street, she does, till she can't see me no more. Never takes her eyes off me. But she knows. Don't trust me far as she can fuckin throw me these days. When I tell her what I done at school, tests and stuff, all bollocks of course, she just raises her eyebrows and shakes her head. Can't get nothing past my mum. But she can't do nothing about it, see. What with Becky bein at school, and Dad still on the dole and miserable as fuck, and her workin all the time, as well as takin in other people's ironin, she's got enough on her plate to bother with me. Not that I fuckin care. Ain't like I need her no more or nothing. Not like what I used to. Me, I don't need fuckin no one.

And the country's all goin tits up. Turns out Dad losin his job was just the tip of the fuckin iceberg. Now there's blokes losin their jobs left, right and fuckin centre, and every other bastard's on strike. There's black rubbish bags pilin up the streets, bodies pilin up the graveyards, and the Army's drivin round in green fire engines. Talk is, we'll even have a woman fuckin Prime Minister soon. Dad reckons Thatcher's more of a geezer than most of the blokes down the boozer. Fuckin hates her, he does. Only thing that gets him riled up nowadays. Mum reckons it'd be great if there's a bird in charge for a change, but she can't stand the old bitch, just like everyone else round here. Dad says she'll rip the country in half before she's done. Seems like no bastard's gonna be helpin me out in the fuckin short term then. Or Keith or Thommo. Even Dad, come to that.

Dad ain't got much of a clue of nothing no more. He's been on the dole nearly two years, and it's a nightmare seein him like this. Mum's aged ten years since Dad stopped work, and he's gone double that. Even got bits of grey in his quiff. It's like overnight he's turned into this old man. Sits in his chair starin at the telly all day. Watches anything. News, soaps, kid's programmes, cartoons, Open bloody University. Don't seem to matter what. Don't even get off his arse to have his tea at the table with the rest of us no more. Eats it off a tray sat in his chair.

Mum takes him down the doctor's regular. Bathroom cupboard's full of tablets and pumps and shit. He ain't supposed to drink, but he does. Keeps him quiet. Drinks and watches telly. That's all he does. He goes down the boozer once a week, on a Friday, with

Uncle Derek which gives us all a fuckin break. That's where he got his tray.

Not even the football cheers him up no more. We still ain't out the Second Division, and don't look likely this season neither. Half the players been sold off and the new ones ain't much cop. And Swansea, Shrewsbury and Orient ain't a patch on Man. U. or Arsenal. Gets Dad out the house every couple of weeks, but that's about it. Keith and Thommo come with us every now and then. Keith's right into it but ain't got the money to come all the time. Thommo, he just comes for the laughs. Not that there's much of them to be had neither.

But we're through to the fourth round of the Cup. Only thing perks Dad up, talkin about the Cup. Says he got a funny feelin about it this year, reckons we've got a right chance. We all think he's talkin out his arse, obviously, but there's this look in his eyes when he says about it that sort of sticks and I can't take me eyes off him. Might be cos he's stoned off his nut what with all them tablets he's on, but it's like somewhere in there, behind those half closed, bloodshot eyes of his, I can see him again. The same old dad I love so fuckin much.

But he's so up and down, I can't fuckin stand it, so I'm out most evenin's soon as tea's done. Ridin me bike, or nippin round Keith or Thommo's. Most times we end up over the Barmy just hangin about. Borin as fuck but it beats bein indoors. Dunno what Becky makes of it all. It's like she don't even notice there's anything wrong. Runs up to Dad whenever she sees him. Arms right round him. Sometimes he don't even touch her, but when he does, you know, when he holds her to him or ruffles her hair, I know he's back. For a bit, anyway.

And I look at Mum and she's all tearin up and I know she'd give anything to have him back the way he was. Sometimes, I think it's only Becky keeps us all goin.

And the Hammers.

We've beat Swansea in the fifth round. Scraped through in the last ten minutes with goals from Psycho and little Paul Allen. But when we draw Villa next, we know we're fucked. Million miles from the likes of us and Swansea, Villa are. A proper fuckin team. First Division. And there's us, mid-table Second. But we're at home, at The Boleyn, and as it's gettin closer, I'm beginnin to think we might have half a chance, you know, if they play really shit and we have a blinder. But that's the only chance we fuckin got.

Ground's packed. Thirty-six thousand. Me and Dad's in the Chicken Run, like usual, and we can't fuckin move, other than clap our hands and jump up and down a bit. Like I says, Villa are good, and none of us think we got a fuckin hope, other than Dad, of course. But I know we'll give it a go. And we do. We match em all over the park. Then in the last minute, just when it looks like we're gonna be listenin to the replay at home on the radio, we get a penalty. A fuckin penalty. None of us got no doubt Tonka's gonna smash it in. And he does.

When the final whistle goes it's panda-fuckin-monium.

And everyone's takin notice now. There's us thinkin Dad's been talkin bollocks all this time, off his fuckin rocker on his tablets, and now we're in the Semis. The fuckin Semis. We got Everton. Still, coulda been worse. The other Semi's Liverpool-Arsenal, so least we didn't get none of them.

Ain't lookin too rosy though, leadin up. We've only won one out the last eight. That was Orient, couple weeks back. And they're shit. Still, might be our name writ on the cup, like Dad says. You never know.

First game against Everton's nil-nil, so I'm thinkin we've least took em to a replay. Gotta be happy with that. And it weren't no fuckin fluke neither, accordin to reports. Replay's up at Leeds. Dirty cheatin cunts.

Mum's out with Becky when the game kicks off, gettin some shoes or something, but the rest of us is all here, sittin round the radio. Me, Dad, Auntie Gwen, Auntie Ivy. Uncle Derek knows the rules, and he's at home. It's close. Fuckin close. One-all with a couple minutes left. And it's soundin like another replay, when the fuckin unbelievable happens.

Cross comes over, and who's in the box? Only Frank fuckin Lampard.

'What the fuck's he doin up there?' Dad says.

And I'm thinkin the same, thinkin he should be back defendin case we get broke on or something. Seconds later, we're both munchin on our fuckin words cos Lamps has launched himself at this ball. Divin header. BANG. Fuckin BANG. Get in there. Geezer on the radio said it was like a fuckin rocket. Keeper had no chance. Whistle goes not long after and, fuck me, we're in the final. And when that whistle went, it was like Dad cracked out his shell or something, like he just come back from wherever he's been last few years.

We watched it all on Match of the Day later. Funny thing, when he scored, Lamps hadn't got a fuckin clue what to do. So he just stands there, then he runs to the fuckin corner flag and does this little fuckin dance round it. Me and Dad's killin ourselves watchin it. Then Dad gets up and does a little shimmy round the lampstand. Silly bastard. Mind you, he only does a few seconds before he falls down in his chair, fucked with the effort. Big grin on his face, red as a fuckin beetroot.

I got the feelin this is as good as it's gettin for us. Our greatest moment – winnin the Semis. And as I'm watchin Dad takin another turn round the lampstand, I'm hopin he's thinkin the same. Fuckin hate for him to have his hopes up on this one.

Like I said, the other Semi's Arsenal-Liverpool, so either way, we're fucked. Arsenal win after three replays. They beat United in last year's final so they're goin for two in a row. We ain't got a hope in fuckin hell against them.

After the Semi, it's like Dad's a changed man. Got his old energy back. Up and lookin for work most days, jokin and laughin. But I fear the fuckin worst. Week before the Cup Final, and it's like it ain't even entered his head we're gonna get slaughtered.

We beat Charlton four-one last game of the season and finish seventh. Arsenal finish fourth from the top of the league, a point behind United. And they're in the final of the Cup Winners' Cup a few days after they play us. No one's givin us a chance. Telly, papers, no one. No one other than my dad, that is. He reckons we're gonna stuff em. Three days to go, he's deckin out the house in claret and blue, laughin and jokin and fallin off ladders like old times. On top of the world, he is, headin for a big fuckin fall.

We're windin paper chains round the bannisters, me and Dad, night before the match, when Mum calls us in from the front room in her 'someone's in for a bollockin' voice.

I'm thinkin what I might have done, apart from the usual, and reckon she might have tumbled me thievin or me smokin. Dad looks at me with the same look I'm givin him. Sheer fuckin terror. We both go in and sit on the settee, hangin our heads like naughty schoolboys.

Mum's standin by the settee, but neither one of us is lookin at her. 'Bill,' she says.

Dad looks up at her and so do I. She gives him an envelope, and she's got tears in her eyes and the biggest smile on her face.

'Go on, dear,' she says. 'Open it up.'

Tears comin down her face now.

'I was puttin some money aside. Just in case.'

She leans over and kisses him on the top of the head.

And he opens the envelope up and pulls out two tickets for the Cup Final. He looks up at her, sort of lost.

Then I realise while all the rest of em, all the rest of us, was takin the piss out of Dad all them times, laughin at him, thinkin what a stupid bastard he was for believin, Mum's savin up every penny she's got. She musta seen that same look in his eyes I see. But where I see the silly old sod I miss so much, she was seein the only man she ever loved.

CHAPTER THIRTEEN

Auntie Ivy's comin over to watch the match on the telly. So's Uncle Derek and Auntie Gwen. Bein Spurs, Uncle Derek hates Arsenal more than the rest of us, so Dad says he can be an honourable Hammer for the day, so long as he leaves his Spurs shirt at home.

Me and Dad's gettin our last orders off Mum.

'Have you had your tablets, Bill?'

'Yes, dear.'

'And you've got your pump with you, just in case?'

'Yes, dear.'

'Good. Now just don't you go getting too excited, love, remember what the doctor said?'

It's like she's talkin to Becky or something, but Dad don't care. Not today. This is the greatest day of his life.

'I've done you up some sandwiches, just to keep you going. Cheese for you, John, and Bill, you've got ham and pickle.'

She hands me a carrier bag. Weighs a tonne. Reckon you can feed half the Chicken Run with this lot.

'And make sure you both have plenty to drink. The weatherman said it's going to be scorcher.'

'Yes, Mum,' me and Dad say together.

It's eleven o'clock already and we want to get goin.

'And boys?'

Fuck me, what now?

Mum smiles big and lovely.

'Have a great time,' she says. 'We'll be looking out for you on the telly, won't we Becky?'

Becky smiles just like Mum and nods her head. Then she runs up and grabs Dad round the legs.

'Wave to me on the telly, Daddy. Wave to me.'

Even though I know he's breakin his neck to get out the door, Dad picks her up and gives her a big squeeze.

'Course I will, darlin. Wouldn't not do that, now, would I?'

He gives Becky a kiss on the head and puts her down. She runs back to Mum, takin the hand Mum's put out for her. Then Dad, slow as you like, does the few steps to Mum and gives her a kiss on the cheek, and whispers something in her ear. Dunno what he says, but Mum's blushin all over and her eyes are fillin right up.

* * *

We're out in the street now, headin fast as we can for the station before Mum calls us back for something else. Reckon it's a million degrees out here. We both got our scarves on. Mine's round me waist but Dad's got his good and proper round his neck. He must be pissin sweat.

The whole street's got flags out windows and scarves round lamposts and we're gettin waves from everyone we know. It's like we was actually playin the way everyone's wishin us good luck and pattin us on the back. Dad's lappin it up. Me, I'm too fuckin nervous to think.

There's a geezer sellin Cup Final bits off a wallpaper table outside the station. Dad gets us a rosette each, and one for Becky, which he stuffs in the carrier bag with the sandwiches. He pins mine on like he's givin me the Victoria fuckin Cross or something. Then he pins his on and flattens the ribbons with his hand and blows his cheeks out. It's like he's just realised we're actually goin to the Cup Final, you know, like it's only just hit him.

'Come on, son,' he says. 'Time for a swift one.'

That means a stop off at The Queen's on Green Street, just outside Upton Park Station. It's only a couple up from Bethnal Green and it's where we go before every home game. Mum don't know. If she ever found out Dad took me anywhere near a boozer, she'd do her bollocks. Fuckin kill him, she would.

Dad's been takin me in The Queen's last couple of seasons before every game. It's a proper Hammers pub. No away supporters in here. Wouldn't bleedin dare. He started me off on coke the year we got relegated, then this year he's upped it to half a shandy. What he don't know is, me and Keith and Thommo been bang on the cider since I was thirteen. Thommo nicks it out his old man's shed. Dad's got this thing about buyin me first pint, like it really means something to him, so I don't let on or nothing.

Upton Park Station's crawlin with Old Bill. All over the gaff. No surprise, really. Arsenal ain't like Millwall, or Uncle Derek's Yids, but there still ain't no fuckin love lost, if you know what I mean.

Green Street's jammed. And the boozer, you can't hardly get near it. Looks like everyone's had the same idea. As we're pushin through the crowds outside, I get a tap on me shoulder. But it ain't a tap it's more like a thump and whoever done it smells of beer and piss. Dribblin Albert, if I had to guess. He's one of Dad's mates from his days at the factory. Collars us every fuckin time.

Now he ain't called Dribblin Albert cos he used to be a fleet footed wizard on the wing in his youth or nothing. He's called Dribblin Albert cos he dribbles. Jaw's fucked. All pushed over one side. Born like it, I should reckon. Dribbles when he's talkin, dribbles when he ain't. Forever moppin it off his chin. Makes this sort of suckin noise when he drinks. And when he's eatin, fuck me, there's a sight you don't wanna see. I know he can't help it but, you know, it ain't fuckin pleasant.

I turn round, and there he is. Huge and hairy and smashed off his face.

'All right, shun. Howsha doin?'

Dad turns round.

'Albert, mate. How's tricks?'

'Heesh growin, your lad, Bill. Gesh bigger every time I shee im.'

He only saw us last week, before the Charlton game. Daft old bastard.

'He is an all, Albert. Gonna be a big lad, ain't ya, John?'

Fuckin hell. This ain't gonna get us a drink. And I'm bleedin parched.

'How long's it been like this, Albert?' Dad says, makin a sort of narky face, lookin at the crowd from here to the bar.

Albert's got no idea what Dad's talkin about. He's sort of fazed out for a moment and he's wobblin a bit.

'All this lot, Albert, how long's they been here?'

'You wanna drink, Bill?' Albert says, comin back to Earth. 'And yer boy, washeewan?'

'Cheers, Albert, mate. Pint of Best for me, and half a shandy for the boy.'

With that, Albert shoves his way past us and everyone else like they ain't there. Me and Dad wait outside. Albert's back ten minutes later with the drinks. Dad reckons the beer's been watered down, but he's soon on his third. Albert's had more than double that, lookin at the state of him, and he's still goin.

'So, washa reckon, Bill? Fink we'll do it?'

Albert's talkin like someone who knows what he should be sayin but ain't got no fuckin idea what he's on about.

'Well,' Dad says, sippin his pint of watered-down gnat's piss, 'no fuckin way it's gonna be easy, mate. But it's the Cup Final, you know. David versus Goliath. Us against the fuckin world. And we got Bonzo, so there ain't no way we're givin up without a fuckin fight.'

And Dad and me and Albert raise a glass to the great Billy Bonds. West Ham through and through. A fuckin hero.

Dad carries on.

'Do em on the break, I reckon,' he says, suddenly all sure of himself. 'One-nil, two-one tops. Yes, Albert, my son, course we can fuckin do it.'

Looks like Albert's got tears in his eyes, but it's probably just years of bein on the piss. Or an eye infection or something.

'COME ON, YOU FUCKIN HAMMERSH!' Albert shouts, like he's just sat on something. Scares the shit out of me and nearly has the whole table over.

Cheers go up all round us and before you know it, there's two hundred pissed up Hammers singin.

It's like they all forgot who we're playin today. Who we're actually up against here. Arsenal. Fuckin Arsenal. It's their third Cup Final in the last three years. And they got Liam Brady. Liam fuckin Brady, for fuck's sake. And who we got up against him? Who we got to keep him quiet, play him off the park? Little Paul Allen. Seventeen years old. A year older than me, and he's got to mark Liam Brady out the game or we're proper fucked.

I've made me mind up. We ain't got no fuckin chance. No fuckin way. But then I look round at all of these blokes around me, all of em singin and I look at me dad and I look at Dribblin Albert, and part of me wonders, you know. Wonders if we really could nick it, just like my dad says.

Dribblin Albert slips off his stool.

Time to go.

**

Me and Dad go through the line of Old Bill outside Upton Park Station, and they don't give us a second look. They're busy with some lads what've tried jumpin the barriers and are cuffin one of em against a wall. Of all the fuckin days to get nicked. No fuckin brains some people.

Trains crammed full of Hammers. No Arsenal nowhere. But when we get out at Wembley Park, we see em. Thousands of em in their red and white shirts and flags and everything. Fuckin thousands of em.

We follow the crowds down Wembley Way, past the hot-dog stands and the programme sellers and the ticket touts. Dad stops for a programme, but Mum'd kill us if we don't eat her sarnies, so the hot-dogs ain't got no hope. Dad's sort of marchin and it's hard to keep up. And as we come up the hill, there it is. Wembley Stadium. Fuck me, it's enormous. Like one of them gigantic wotsit things in Roman times with gladiators and lions and all that shit.

And the crowd's all backed up, tryin to get in. I get Dad to look at our tickets to see what turnstile we need. We're right round the other side, so we get marchin again. The further round we get, the more Hammers we see, until that's all there is. A sea of Hammers. And it's fuckin beautiful.

I remember me first game at the Boleyn. That feelin when you walk up the steps and it all opens out before you. Near took me breath away as a littl'un. But Wembley? There ain't nothing like Wembley, not in the whole fuckin world. Place is fillin up already and there's still a couple of hours to kick-off. By then, there'll be hundred thousand in here. Hundred fuckin thousand.

We're behind the goal. All Mum could get, I reckon. Not great, but what's not great about bein here? Fuckin nothing. I'm lookin at the programme, and Dad's lookin round the place like he just fell out the sky.

Bonzo and the lads are out on the pitch all suited up. They walk behind the goal and we all stand and clap as one. And they look so small. They give us a clap back and walk round to where the rest of the Hammers are round the side.

Brass band's out, marchin up and down, playin brass band shit. Then they stop in the middle of the pitch, all still, and start playin Abide With Me. I quickly turn to the bottom of page two in the programme where they've writ the words, and me and Dad sing it out together. Every man around us is singin hard. All readin the words off the programme so you can tell not a fuckin one of us goes to church or nothing. But here they are. Here we are. Men. Singin for our lives.

'Abide with me; fast falls the eventide;
The darkness deepens, Lord with me abide;
When other helpers fail; and comforts flee;
Help of the helpless; O abide with me.'

I'm so choked at the end of that first verse, can't barely get through the next one what with the tears runnin down me face. Dad's the same, and for the rest of the singin, we're just holdin on to each other. Man and boy. Father and son.

I hope to God we win. Hope to fuckin God. Can't stand to think what it'd do to Dad if we don't. See, when you're watchin it on telly or listenin to it on the radio, you can just turn it off. Kill the feelin.

But when you're here, you're part of it, and it gets so it's a part of you. And there ain't nowhere you can fuckin hide.

***

A roar goes up right round the ground, like the sound of a buildin comin down. And here they come. Looks like we lost the toss for kits cos we've come out in our away kit. All white with light blue trim. Bit poofy, but we can't do nothing about that now. Dunno why, but Arsenal's wearin their away kit an all. Yellow shirts, blue shorts. About level as far as the poofy stakes go, but I reckon we might just've nicked it.

Everyone's lined up, and Bonzo's takin some suited up geezer to shake hands with our lads. Paul Allen looks littler than Becky, and the Arsenal look so fuckin huge, sort of steady, like they know all they gotta do is turn up. And it ain't just me wonderin why Johnny Lyall's playin Psycho up front on his own. I mean, one up against the Arsenal. We ain't got no chance of fuckin scorin with that.

Me heart's batterin me on the inside, hurtin. And I got Dad tremblin right next to me, closer than skin.

Whistle blows.

Here we go.

CHAPTER FOURTEEN

Arsenal kick off. Fourteen passes later, we still ain't had a fuckin touch. The bloke standin next to me's shakin his head.

'Men against boys,' he says, loud enough for more than me to hear. 'Men against fucking boys.'

Someone behind shouts at him to stop bein a prick, and he shuts up. Dad gives me a nudge.

'Don't worry, son,' he says, 'you wait till we get goin. We'll show em.'

Graham Rix lumps the ball up to Liam Brady, and he's offside. Free kick. Bonzo knocks it back to big Phil Parkes in our goal, and he's bouncin the ball about, rollin it round in his hands. A chant of 'Come on you Irons' goes up all round us, and me and Dad join in. The bloke next me, he's quiet as a fuckin mouse.

And we grow. We start knockin it about. Brooking's lookin class in the middle, little Paul Allen's scrappin round him like a fuckin terrier and Pikey's pickin up all the loose balls. Devo's killin em every time he gets it. Dancin round em, he is. And when Arsenal do get forward, Bonzo and Alvin Martin are slammin the door shut right in their faces and gettin it back to Parkesy easy as you like.

Psycho has a shot from twenty five yards, but it's shit and bounces through to Pat Jennings in the Arsenal goal. The miserable bastard next to me's shoutin to have Psycho took off, but a chorus of Bubbles drowns the fucker.

'Unlucky, Psycho, mate. Keep it goin!'

And Arsenal, fuck, they don't look up for it at all. I know it's bloody hot down there, but they're just strollin about. When they do get it, they're passin it sidewards or back, and we're chasin em down wherever they are. Fuck, you'd think it was us the First Division side at the moment. I take me eyes off the game for a few seconds and look round behind me at all the tens of thousands of Hammers singin and shoutin and wavin their flags, and I wanna fuckin cry.

Then there's a rumble and a roar, and everyone round me's strainin to see. Stuart Pearson's picked the ball up in the middle of the park. He's darted between two of their defenders, and he's left em for dead.

'Come on, Stu, come on, son!'

Even the bloke next to me's willin him on.

'Make it a good un, Pearson,' he yells, more like a schoolteacher than a football fan.

Pearson cuts the ball back, and it's come to one of ours. Can't see who it is cos there's so many people up in front of me. Then, through a break in the heads, I see it's Geoff fuckin Pike. Pikey. Runs all fuckin day, he does, but he ain't gonna score in a million fuckin years. But he hits it first time, and it ain't fuckin bad, as it goes. *Come on.* Flies through a crowd of players, but Jennings dives on it. First proper shot of the game to us, though, and we got em fuckin rattled.

'Unlucky, Pikey,' my old man shouts out. 'Keep it goin, son!'

'Unlucky?' the bloke next to me says, like he's talkin to everyone and no one at all. 'Unlucky? Look at the space he was in. Should've took it wide and pinged it across. Shooting from there? Fucking idiot.'

But Dad don't hear him. He's too busy shoutin and encouragin and kickin every fuckin ball. But he's needlin me, this other fella. Really fuckin needlin me.

Brooking picks the ball up just inside the Arsenal half, and he bobbles it wide to Devo. Devo skins two Arsenal players, and goes wide. We're fillin the box; Psycho, Stuart Pearson, even Lamps and Brooking. Arsenal's all over the place. It's a decent ball in, Jennings pushes it away, comes to Psycho, he shoots, comes off an Arsenal defender, out to Pearson, he has a bang and it's gone across the goal and Brooking's fell on his arse, but his got his head to it and . . .

'YEEEEEEEEEEEEEEEESSSSSSSSSSSSSSSS!!!!!!!!!!!!!!'

Fuckin mental. Everyone's jumpin up and down, jumpin on each other, punchin the air. Dad's standin straight, clappin his hands raw, and his eyes are bulgin and the veins in his neck are stickin out. And I know he's too choked to even speak. Miserable fucker next to me's been jumped by about eight blokes all rufflin his hair and kissin his head. I can't see fuck all in front, not with all this goin on, but it's fuckin brilliant. Thirteen minutes in and we're one-nil up against the mighty fuckin Arsenal. Who would've fuckin though it?

I think of Mum and Becky, and everyone, watchin the game back home, and I bet they're fuckin jumpin all over the gaff. Especially Uncle Derek. I bet he's fuckin pissin himself.

Steward comes over and tells us all to calm down. No one takes a blind bit of notice and the fucker slides away. Rest of the half,

Arsenal don't do nothing. Parkesy ain't had a save to make and Bonzo and Alvin Martin's winnin it all at the back. The Arsenal can't get hold of Devo at all, and little Paul Allen's still flyin into em all over the park.

Half-time whistle goes. One-nil.

Durin half-time, me and Dad don't talk about the winnin. It's like if we talk about it, we'll fuckin jinx it. He's just lookin round, lookin at all the flags wavin and lookin at the massive scoreboard, and at the green lines on the pitch. He looks up to the Royal Box on the halfway line and stays there. That's where Bonzo's gonna lift the cup if we hold on. And I know Dad's seein it now, in his head, like we've already won it.

I'm lookin for Mum's sarnies, and see em all scattered under everyone's feet in front, trampled to fuck. Must've happened when we scored. I get the programme out and have a read. The bloke next to me's tryin to tell me we're in for a right bashin second half. I wanna tell him to fuck off, but I can't be fuckin bothered. Besides, he could be fuckin right.

Teams are back out and the second half gets goin. It's all Arsenal. They've obviously had a right fuckin rocket up their arses at half-time, and they're proper up for it.

A smoke bomb comes out the Arsenal end and lands on the side of the pitch. Forty thousand Hammers start singin 'Just because you're losin', and it gets us away from the fact Arsenal's all over us.

Alan Sunderland's got the ball, slides it to Rix. Rix does two of our players, cuts inside and curls the ball low at the goal. Fuck. It's on target. Big Phil Parkes looks too far away to get to it, but he flings himself full length and tips it round the post. First real shot they've had in the whole game. We gotta stay strong first twenty cos if we don't, they're gonna fuckin slaughter us.

We know we're in a proper fuckin game now. But Bonzo and Alvin are still winnin everything in the air, and Paul Allen's runnin his little legs off. But we're gettin pinned back all over. No fuckin gettin away from it. Only a matter of time. Dad don't stop shoutin and encouragin, though, and he's singin his heart out the whole time. He's kickin every ball out there. And the heat's gettin worse and worse.

Liam Brady skins Frankie Lampard. Different player this half, Brady. Different fuckin player. Puts in a dangerous cross, and Devo miscontrols it for a corner. Shit. But it's all right cos Parkesy's come out and caught it no fuckin problem.

'COME ON YOU IRONS! COME ON YOU IRONS!'

Every time we get rid of the ball, Arsenal's bringin it straight back. But they're not hurtin us. Not really. They got loads of the ball, but they ain't really doin nothing with it, and the longer it goes on the more fucked they're gonna get in this heat.

Halfway through the second half. Still one-nil.

Sammy Nelson comes on for them. Looks like Marty Feldman.

Brady's gone down on the edge of the box. Fuckin dodgy, this. Wall's lined up. Brady knocks it to Talbot who bangs it first time. It's headin for the top corner but Parkesy comes out of nowhere and plucks it out the air. Fuckin had me heart in me mouth on that one.

We break quick. Devo's goin down the wing. Plays it inside to Paul Allen. Beats one, shoots. Fuckin rubbish. Still, that's another few minutes gone. I look at me watch and tell Dad there's about twenty left. He nods, but he don't say a word. It's like if he comes down from wherever he is, it'll break some sort of spell or something, and the whole lot'll come crashin down.

Feelin's goin round like we can really fuckin do this. There's like a real buzz gettin up, and me and Dad are singin Bubbles with every other Hammer in the ground.

And we're startin to look all right. They're runnin out of ideas, and we're holdin our own, and Bonzo's havin a fuckin blinder. Alvin Martin's gone up for a header and goes down, holdin his head. That's all we fuckin need. He's down for a good few minutes. I ask Dad if he reckons we'll bring Brushy on, cos I see him warmin up. Dad don't hear me. It's like he's a thousand miles away, lost in it all.

Alvin's back on his feet, thank fuck. Scouser. Hard bastard. It'll take more than a bash in the face to keep him down.

The game carries on, and they're pinnin us back again. Fifteen to go. Rix does four of ours in one hit and gets brought down on the edge. Free kick comes to nothing. We gotta stop givin the fuckin ball away. We're just lumpin it forward now, and all it's doin is comin straight back. But Arsenal are lookin fucked, and their fans have gone all quiet. We're sufferin an all, mind. Psycho's dead on his feet and Alvin looks like he don't even know what day of the fuckin week it is. Mind you, like I says, he is a Scouser so he probably struggles with that sort of thing the best of fuckin times.

Last ten and Pikey's got the ball thirty yards out. He's standin still, waitin for one of the Arsenal defenders to make a move. When they do, he breaks forward, edge of the box. We're all watchin. Waitin. Shoots. Right foot. What a load of shit.

Both teams look fucked now. It's so hot, and there ain't no air at all up here so fuck knows what it's like down there. It's like the fifteenth round of a heavyweight fight. Most of the players on both sides look like they're in slow motion. Then from nowhere, Bonzo's harin down the left wing. Crosses. And Tonka, of all fuckin people's in the middle. Gets in front of Jennings, spins and shoots. Comes off the keeper. Has another pop. Fizzles out.

Then they're comin back at us. Psycho's give it away on the edge of the box, Stapleton's goin through, but Bonzo and Alvin make two fantastic tackles, each of em flyin in like they're playin for their fuckin lives.

The whole game's opened up now. End to end. Five minutes left. They've got a corner, but Pearson's got hold of it and Paul Allen belts it out fifty yards. But it comes straight back like it's been doin the whole half.

Now Frankie Lampard's got it on the left. He's runnin over the halfway line. Gives it to Devo who gives it to Brooking. Brooking knocks it to Paul Allen goin like a fuckin train. He's on the last defender. Slips the ball through his legs, and he's comin to the edge of the box. Pat Jennings is off his line. Everyone round me, everyone's cranin their necks, strainin to see. If he bangs this in, there ain't no comin back.

He's eighteen months older than me, Paul Allen. Seventeen and a bit. And he don't even know he's carryin the hopes of all of us in his hands, in his feet.

'Go on, my son,' I scream. 'Go on, my fuckin son.'

And he's about to win us the cup. It's like everything's gone quiet and sort of slowed down. The bloke next to me's got his fists clenched and grittin his teeth. I'm jumpin up and tryin to see over the heads in front, then . . .

CRUNCH.

Willy Young, that lanky streak of ginger Scotch piss, the Arsenal centre back, takes little Paul Allen's fuckin legs away. Cuts him right in half. Paul's in a heap on the edge of the box. My dad's goin mental. All of us are. And fuckin right. See, to be West Ham means something. Means something more than football. We're hard, I mean with Bonzo and Tonka and Alvin Martin, they're three fuckers you don't mess with. But we're fair. And fair means the fuckin world. The people round here, the people of the East End, we don't turn no one over, and if we do, and we get caught, we hold our fuckin hands up. We ain't afraid of a bit of fuckin graftin, if that's what it takes. We do what fuckin needs to be done. And if we fuck up, we hold our fuckin hands up to that an all. So when little

Paul Allen gets chopped in half by that ginger streak of Scotch piss it goes against everything. All of it.

Little Paul's up on his feet again, no rollin about, no play-actin, no nothing. Just gets up. Greatest moment of his life, and he just gets up, dusts himself down, and carries on. Top fuckin geezer.

Even in the last couple of minutes we're not lookin to run the clock down or nothing or time-wastin, and shit. We keep comin at em. Geezer next to me's yellin to stick it in the corners, and for once, he makes a bit of fuckin sense. But it ain't us. It ain't the West Ham way.

I can fuckin taste it now. Fuck knows what Dad's goin through. He ain't said nothin to me since half-time. World of his own. Face is all flushed, and those veins are stickin out his neck like a fuckin roadmap.

Clock says fifteen seconds. Brady lumps it forward. Dad's grabbin hold of me arm till he's nearly pullin me over.

He knows it's nearly time.

AND THERE IT IS!!!!!!!!!!!!!!!!!!!!

Psycho's on his knees, Brooking's down, and big Phil Parkes is layin flat on his face in the goal. Geezer next to me's huggin the bloke behind him, there's flags flyin and people shoutin, and I wanna hug my Dad.

I turn round, and he ain't right, got this sort of pleadin look on him. His face is gone mauve and it's all tight, and he's got his hands clutchin his chest.

'Dad! Dad!'

I'm tryin to get to him, but in all the chaos of winnin he's movin further away, like he's bein washed out to sea.

'Dad! Dad!'

There's a line of stewards in the aisle about twenty yards off. I start shoutin to em, but they don't even turn round. Dad's sinkin and the shine in his eyes is floatin away.

I'm crawlin on me hands and knees towards him, and when I get there, I hold him to me and think of Mum watchin Bonzo liftin the cup on telly, and I know she's thinkin of us, me and Dad, and thinkin how happy we'll be. And someone's brought a steward over, and a St. John's Ambulance geezer's tryin to talk to me but I ain't listenin, and I'm pushin him off cos I ain't lettin him take my dad.

CHAPTER FIFTEEN

Day of the funeral comes round quick, and it's like I ain't even had time to make any of it real. Fuckin none of it. All that's stuck in me head's the Hammers players goin down at the end of the match like they been shot, and the look on that steward's face as he's comin over to see Dad. Don't remember nothing else.

All the papers and the telly next day and all fuckin week is full of pictures of little Paul Allen pickin up his medal and sobbin his heart out goin down the Wembley steps. Me, I couldn't care a fuck no more. There's a bit in the locals about Dad. Nothing much. Fuckin bastards even got his name wrong.

Mum's in me bedroom helpin me with this tie I been fightin with for ages. She does it up quick as anything. Sort of mechanical, like. The doorbell rings. Shit. Mum said the car wouldn't be here for another half hour. Suddenly I feel sick, like I wanna hide under me bed and never come out. Mum sees it in me eyes and gives me a big hug. Her face is all hot, and she tries whisperin something in me ear but nothing comes out. She lets go of me and blows her cheeks out, and looks at the floor.

'It'll be all right, love,' she says, and looks at me and tries to smile, but it nearly breaks her.

The doorbell rings again. Mum goes without a word, and I see her cover her mouth with her hand as she goes to the top of the stairs.

I sit on me bed. *Hold it in, son, hold it in.* A few minutes later, Mum's comin back up the stairs. I squeeze the end of me nose till it hurts and hold me breath, then stand back up as if I been standin there the whole time.

'It's only Mrs Jessup, love,' Mum says, quiet, like, and gets me jacket out the wardrobe. 'I've left her in the kitchen making a cuppa.'

Mad Mrs Jessup's lookin after Becky while me an Mum's at the funeral. Mum told me I don't have to go, but she ain't pullin that 'you're only a kid' shit on me. He was my dad. My fuckin dad.

Fuck, this is hard.

Thommo's give me this jacket he had for his nan's funeral. It ain't a bad one. Fits all right. There was all these stains down the bottom of the arms where he'd been wipin his eyes and cuffin his snot, but Mum got em out okay. She puts it on me, brushes the shoulders down and pulls the front together. Then she stands back to have a look. Her eyes get all filled up and she puts her hand over her mouth again.

'Oh, John,' she says, and the tears start floodin.

She's like this all the bloody time. One minute, looks like she's all right, next, she's fuckin fallin apart. I wanna put me arms round her when she's like this. Tell her everything's gonna be all right. But I know nothing's gonna be the same again. Not ever. How the fuck can it be? So, I don't even move towards her. Just sit down on me bed and look at me hands.

Becky's downstairs gigglin at cartoons. She knows what's happened to Dad. Mum told her. Fuckin never thought I'd get through that, Mum tellin Becky her dad's dead, and then breakin down and Becky comin over and tellin Mum she loves her. She's took it better than all of us. It's like she knows Dad's all right, or something, like somehow he's really fuckin okay. It's like she ain't clicked he ain't never comin back.

Mum's sorted herself out now, and blows her cheeks out and dabs the tears off her face with a tissue.

'Tea's ready, dears,' Mrs Jessup shouts from downstairs, the mad old bat.

'Come on, John,' Mum says, tryin to grab hold of me hand to go down with her.

As if a cuppa's gonna make a blind bit of fuckin difference. I got both me fists clenched and I'm lookin straight at her. And me nails are diggin in me hands, and it fuckin hurts, and the pain's the only thing keepin me from bawlin me fuckin eyes out. I tell her I'll be down in a minute, and she goes. Then I go in the bathroom and throw up in the sink.

***

London Crematorium, Aldersbrook Road. It's took us fuckin ages gettin here. Big old gaff. Massive gardens and everything. We're in the car behind the one with Dad in. Big fuck-off Merc. Uncle Derek's sorted everything out, cars and shit, flowers, that sort of thing. Him and Auntie Gwen. Auntie Ivy's been worse than Mum. She come round the other day, plonked herself in the front room, cried for fuckin hours, then upped and left. Never said a fuckin word.

As we're gettin out the motor, I see a few people hangin about. There's Tony, runs The Bell, Dad's local. He's laid on a spread after, like what he did with Grandad when he passed. Top bloke, Tony. Salt of the fuckin earth. And fuck me, there's Dribblin Albert. Looks fuckin awful. Worse than normal, if that can be fuckin imagined. He's leant up against a tree, like someone's nailed him to it, lookin at the sky.

And there's loads of other people just waitin. Waitin for us, I suppose. There's geezers from the factory, the boozer, and blokes Dad knew when he went football. Half the street's turned up. A few of em come up to Mum, one or two at a time, say a few bits, and go in the chapel. Even Old Cartwright from next door's here, all suited and booted and wearin his army medals.

Mum don't say nothing back to no one. She's holdin onto me arm so hard it's like she can't stand up by herself. People start disappearing inside till there's just me and Mum, Auntie Gwen, Auntie Ivy, and Uncle Derek. And then these geezers come round the corner carryin Dad's coffin. Mum leans in and starts bawlin on me shoulder. Starts Auntie Ivy off, and I'm hangin onto the both of em, one on each fuckin arm. Uncle Derek comes over and grabs Auntie Ivy off me, thank fuck, then one of the coffin geezers asks if we're ready. Uncle Derek says we are, and the coffin gets carried in. Then he nods at me to go in after it, and gives me this look as if I should fuckin know.

But I ain't never been to no fuckin funeral, cunt. I ain't got no fuckin idea what happens. Not a fuckin clue. I'm fifteen fuckin years old and me dad's dead, all right? So fuck off.

Mum whispers at me to start walkin in. She's draggin on me arm something terrible, and I can only just about pull her along. Dunno where we're supposed to sit. I know the place is packed cos it's pushin down on me from both sides, squeezin me in. I'm keepin me head down, lookin at the floor. And it's like I'm goin through this cold, dark tunnel, one that ain't never gonna end, and if I turn me head, turn me head just once, the whole fuckin thing's gonna come down on top of me.

I lift me head up when we get to the top and there's nowhere else to go. The front row's empty. Must be us. The coffin gets set up in the corner, and I help Mum sit down. Uncle Derek and me two aunties come and sit down after us.

Everything goes quiet, and the vicar starts talkin like he's knowed Dad his whole life. And I wanna hurt him, really fuckin hurt him. And all these bastards. What the fuck they doin here anyway? He weren't their fuckin dad. Got fuck all to do with em.

There's a couple of hymns, and then me Uncle Derek gets up front, says a few words, and I'm sittin here thinkin none of this is fuckin real. I mean, how can that box sittin over there have my dad in it? My dad. I mean, what sort of a fuckin game's that?

And before I know it, it's all finished and they're puttin Dad on a fuckin conveyor belt, like he's a box of corn flakes at Mum's shop. Some geezer somewhere presses a button and the fuckin thing starts movin. Fuckin mental. And Dad goes through the curtain and disappears, like some shit magic trick off the telly.

Mum's stopped cryin for a while when Uncle Derek was talkin, but that curtain thing sets her off again. I put me arm round her. Feels sort of funny, like it ain't me, like I'm not really doin it. And I got Auntie Ivy the other side snottin all over me shoulder. Uncle Derek reaches over and ruffles me head. And I bite the bottom of me lip till it bursts, and the blood's washin round me mouth and it's only the taste of it what's holdin me together.

**

Like I says, Tony's laid on a spread at The Bell after. But I don't want none of that shit, people sayin they're sorry, and what a great bloke Dad was, and how if there's anything they can fuckin do, and all that bollocks. Mum and me, we show our faces then fuck off home. Uncle Derek and me two aunties stay. Reckon Auntie Ivy's gonna drink the fuckin place dry, state she's in. Uncle Derek said at Grandad's she got so pissed she ended up goin in the Gents and passin out in one of the shit-houses.

**

Couple of weeks after the funeral Mum's scrubbin the kitchen down. It's all she does. Scrubs and cleans and makes endless cups of fuckin tea. Becky's back at school, so Mum makes sure she's washed and dressed, and does her packed lunch and drops her off and picks her up. Does me a packed lunch an all, even though she knows I ain't goin school no more. Keeps the house clean and makes sure her kids is all right. Nothing else she can do. She ain't back at work yet. Says she's givin it another couple of weeks.

It's night-time. Becky's asleep upstairs, and I'm sittin in the front room on me own, listenin to Dad's Elvis records. But they don't do nothing for me, not like what they did for him. See, they was his records. Got nothing to do with me. The records I got's hid in the bottom of me wardrobe upstairs. They're all what I nicked when I been out with Thommo and Keith. Ain't never even fuckin listened to em.

And I'm shit scared. And I'm tryin to hold it together, but I can't do this on me own. Keith and Thommo, they're doin their best. They come over most nights, but they dunno what to say. They're just kids emselves. We go over The Barmy, smoke some fags and get pissed on the cheap cider from Thommo's shed. But not one of us says a fuckin word about Dad.

And I wonder how kids like me ever get through shit like this.

'Do you want a cuppa, love?'

'No.'

Mum takes off her Marigolds and comes and sits next to me on the settee. Puts her arm round me. I feel myself flinch. Don't mean to. Just, fuck, I dunno.

'You know, love,' she says, 'whenever you need to talk, whenever you need to let it all out, I'm here. I'm here for you, love. You do know that don't you?'

She gives me shoulder a squeeze and kisses me on the head, like she fuckin understands.

Only one person ever knows what this is like. Only one person I know been through this. And he's the only one I wanna talk to right now. The only one. Thing is, I ain't seen him since they dragged him out the school canteen all them years back after he beat the shit out of that cunt Wilkins with a dinner tray.

Since Mum started full-time down the supermarket, when Dad lost his job, I ain't heard a squeak out of Kenny's old girl. Ain't seen nothing of her neither. Mum goes over pretty regular, though, takes her some dinners, and that. Does a bit of cleanin once a week. But whenever you go past their house, the curtains are always shut, and there's no one comes in or out or nothing. See the lights at night though, and sometimes see the telly goin through the curtains, so she ain't done away with herself yet. Not like the old man, anyways. Mind you, she's probably nutty as a fuckin fruitcake by now.

But seein as I got no idea where Kenny's holed up, I gotta go and see her. I mean, I got no fuckin choice in the matter.

CHAPTER SIXTEEN

I give Mum some spiel about meetin Thommo and Keith somewhere, and head over to Kenny's.

Kenny's gaff's only cross the road, but it's like a million fuckin miles away, like I'm goin back in time and Kenny's lookin out his bedroom window, and his arsehole of an old man's asleep in the chair, and his mum's in the kitchen makin up jam sarnies and lemonade.

I knock, really soft, like I don't really want no one bein in. No answer. Not a peep. I wanna walk away, but I can't. Not fuckin like this.

I knock again. Louder.

The door creaks open, but it's on the latch and all I can see is these eyes squintin through the dark. It's her. Kenny's old girl.

'Kenny?' she says, her voice creakin just like the door she's just opened.

Reeks of fags and booze, she does, and it's like she's holdin onto the door to stop her fallin on her face.

'It's me, Mrs Montgomery. John, across the road.'

She's still squintin at me, tryin to make me out. It ain't like she can't see me proper or nothing. Ain't gonna be dark for a while. Just she's pissed, that's all.

'John?'

'That's right, Mrs Montgomery, from Kenny's class at school.'

It's clear she ain't got a fuckin clue who I am. Then this look sort of flashes cross her face.

Massive smile, she does. Shows all her black and crusted teeth. Fuck me, they're awful.

'Have you come for tea, love?' she says.

Fuckin hell. Away with the fuckin fairies this one.

'That's right, Mrs Montgomery. Come for tea.'

She closes the door a bit to get the chain off and opens it up wide. And, fuck me, she looks like she's just been dug up out the garden. She got a fag hangin out the side of her mouth, an inch of ash crumbling off, and her hair's all stiff and up and all over the fuckin place. She's in this filthy fuckin dressin gown and got lipstick smeared round her mouth and the make-up round her eyes is all comin off on her cheeks where she's been cryin. Gaff stinks of cat shit and piss and sick. I sort of gag, but I cover it up by wipin me nose on the back of me hand. The fag hangin out her mouth's all ash now, and it breaks off, droppin on the carpet and she just walks right over it.

'I'll get you a drink,' she says, but instead of headin for the kitchen, she staggers into the front room, like she's already forgot what she just said.

I follow her in. She's climbed right up one end of this shitty settee, right tight in the corner.

'Sit down, dear. John, did you say?'

'That's right, Mrs Montgomery. From Kenny's class.'

I sit up the other end from her. Nowhere else to sit. Just this settee. Telly's blinkin in the corner. A little black and white portable. The screen's so fuzzy I can't hardly see what's on. Some fuckin quiz show or something, I think. I look round, thinkin there might be a picture of Kenny up somewhere, but there's fuck all. Wallpaper's peelin off the walls, and the carpets stained with patches of piss. Probably the cat. Although, lookin at the state of Kenny's old girl here, I wouldn't put it fuckin past her.

'Would you like a fag, dear?'

A fag? Brings a smile to me face. First time in ages. She's askin me if I'm wantin a fag?

'If you got one,' I say. 'Cheers.'

'I'll just get you one, dear,' she says.

Never turn down a free snout.

After a bit of a struggle, she manages to pull herself off the settee. And as she staggers past, I see she's pissin herself as she's walkin.

She comes back ten minutes later, with a carrier bag.

'I've got them in here somewhere, love,' she says, shovin her hand in the carrier and rummagin around.

But she can't find em and ends up tippin the whole lot on the carpet. There's all sorts of shit in there. Sweet wrappers, old bus tickets, a purse, some letters, couple of stuck together Spangles, and about half a dozen screwed-up fag packets. She looks in all the boxes then puts em back in the bag, sort of lookin surprised every time she finds one of em empty.

I'm watchin her do all this, all this fuckin shit, and wonderin what the fuck I'm still doin here, when she picks up a screwed up bit of paper that's come out the bag. She flattens it out right gentle, like it's something sort of special. I can see it's typed but can't see nothing else. She holds it right up to her eyes and she's readin it, and her mouth's movin, just like what Kenny used to do.

The smell of cat shit's got down me throat and I think I'm gonna throw up. And I ain't gettin no fuckin joy here. I'm just gettin up when she sort of wails. Wails like a proper fuckin banshee. Scares the shit outta me. She's holdin this letter tight to her chest, and bawlin her fuckin eyes out.

Ain't no point stayin. Not with this fuckin lunatic. I've made me mind up, and I'm off. What the fuck was I thinkin anyway? I'm just about to open the front door, when everything goes quiet. She's stopped. She's fuckin stopped. Then it hits me that bit of paper might be something about Kenny. Deep breath, but not too deep, you know, and I go back in the front room.

She's asleep, head nodded forward. Snorin all quiet like a fuckin baby. The bit of paper what she was lookin at's on her lap, under her hands. I sneak over, tryin not to tread in her piss. Wouldn't wanna do that. Not really. I'm nearly there, right in front of her, when she farts and it sort of wakes her up. She sits up straight and snorts then goes straight back to sleep again. It's like playin 'What's the time, Mister fuckin Wolf?' like what we did as kids. I wait a while, but she's out for the fuckin count this time.

I whip the paper off her lap quick as a flash, and I'm gone.

It's got bloody freezin outside, like it does when the sun disappears all of a sudden. The street lamp's just comin on, the same one Kenny spent half his life lookin at. I lean up against the lamp-post and have a gander at the letter. And it is. It's about Kenny. It's from the hospital, some mental place out in Essex. Date's two months back. Says Kenny's too old to stay there, bein a kids' place an all. They want his old girl to come to some sort of meetin. Reckon they can't find nothing else for him. He's much better, so they reckon. Anglin at gettin him home, that's what I think. Well, that obviously ain't fuckin materialised, has it. Like I says, this was two months ago. He could be anywhere now.

Only one thing to do. Old girl's fucked, she ain't gonna be no use. Gotta have me, Keith and Thommo go over Kenny's nut-house, see what the score is. If he ain't there, like if they've moved him some place else or something, we get em to tell us where he's gone and -

Shit. Who the fuck am I kiddin? Three fifteen year old fuckin knobs like us, turn up at a nut-house in the middle of fuckin nowhere, tell em we gotta see Kenny? Fuckin right, they're gonna take some fuckin notice of us, ain't they? And, anyway, what the fuck's the point? Kenny, yeah, he knows what it feels like, but fuckin look at him. Been half his life in a fuckin lunatic asylum. Like he fuckin coped.

I go home, let myself in. Mum's got the telly blarin. Probably don't even hear me come in. Don't wanna see her anyway. Don't even wanna look at her. I sneak upstairs. Me bedroom door's open. Becky's lyin on the floor, colourin. I step over her. She don't move a muscle. Tongue's out the side of her mouth,concentratin too much to notice. I'm steppin over her and headin towards the window.

I look out the garden. Grass a foot high and Dad's flower bed's all gone to shit. Mum hangs the washin out, but apart from that no one goes out the garden no more. I see me old Raleigh Chopper stood up against the back fence, paint peelin off. Brakes are rusty and the gears are fucked

The sun's goin in. And there's shadows. Long, thin, shadows creepin towards me.

BANG

I put me fist through the window.

Blood and glass all over. Becky's screamin and Mum's runnin. And I'm lookin at how the top of me hand's opened right up and how the bits of glass stickin in it look so fuckin beautiful. It's like they've been stuck there me whole life and I've only just noticed.

CHAPTER SEVENTEEN

Uncle Derek has a right pop at me after that stunt with the window. Says I'm the man of the house now and ought to start fuckin actin like one. Gives me a right goin over, he does. And he's right. I know he's right. 'Yes, Uncle Derek,' I says. 'No, Uncle Derek.' Three bags fuckin full, Uncle Derek. And all the time I'm thinkin, Who the fuck do you think you are? Talkin to me like you was fuckin worth pissin on. You Yid cunt.

Me sixteenth birthday comes and goes without so much as a fuckin balloon. Not that I want it all jelly and ice-cream or nothing but, you know, something would have been nice. Mum give me a card with a tenner in it. That was it. A card with a tenner.

'Love, Mum and Becky.'

I pocket the dosh and rip the card to bits.

Keep myself to myself most of the time. And when I get right down, when I get really fuckin low, I got this little penknife what I nicked when I was up west with Keith and Thommo one time. Give me arm a little scratch with it or the top of me leg, or just push the blade as hard as I can without goin in. I got a couple of old scars I open up every now and then when I'm really pissed off, but I always got a smile ready for Mum. And I'm sayin all the right things, makin all the right noises, and she's none the fuckin wiser.

I got me a little part-time job with a mate of Dad's, Charlie Paynter. Charlie's got this fruit and veg stall at Brick Lane, and me and Keith help put it up for him and take it down of a Sunday. Thommo ain't up for it. Too fucked off his face on Evo-Stik to get up that time of the mornin. Half past four, heftin lumps of steel up and down, tryin to bolt it together when your fingers are so cold feels like you ain't fuckin got none. But I like the harshness of it, you know, the cold and the dark. Don't even like no one talkin to me. Just wanna feel the cold and breathe the dark right in.

Good bloke, Charlie, salt of the fuckin earth. I tell Mum I'm savin what Charlie's givin me, cos that's what she wants to hear. But I ain't got a penny to me name. All goes on burgers and kebabs and shit. And there ain't nothing else I want that I can't get by other means, if you know what I'm sayin.

We got the old shopliftin down to a fine art now. Tapes, sweets, tins of beans. Fuckin anything. Thommo's dad, he was inside for a while, he's got this pitch at the market, other end of the Bethnal Green Road. He tells us what he wants, and we get it. Then he flogs it. Don't give us much of a cut, mind, the tight cunt.

But it's gettin so it's a right pain in the arse, you know, like he's really fuckin muggin us off. All right when we first started, we was just kids. It was a bit of a laugh. But we're gettin a few close shaves now. And I'm thinkin it's time to get out.

Last straw come when I'm in this record shop down Bishopsgate not long back. I got me list of tapes what Thommo's old man wants. Like I says, we're nickin to order now, real fuckin professional. Long as you follow the rules it's a piece of piss. Check where the staff is. Have an exit. Just get what you gotta get. And keep your head about you at all fuckin times.

I gotta pick up four tapes; AC/DC, Queen, Deep Purple, Rollin Stones. I got loads more today, but four tapes is all I can get in me coat. Once I've got em, the plan is to drop em off to Thommo waitin round the corner with his big fuck off sports bag. Then it's on to the next gaff.

Place is half empty, makes it a bit harder. But I'm sort of makin me way to the front, pickin up a record here and there, lookin at it for a while, then puttin it back. That's what everyone else is doin, so I know I ain't standin out. There's two blokes behind the counter. One's a fuckin fat-arse, looks about fifty, so he ain't gonna be no trouble, but the other one, he's younger, and he looks like he can shift a bit. I slip Queen in me pocket. One down, three to go.

The fat bloke puts some electronic shit on the record player. OMD or some sort of fuckin rubbish, and he's up there dancin like a cunt behind the counter, like he wants everyone to see him and say what a fuckin laugh he is, what a great fuckin bloke he is, but he ain't. He's just a sad, fat wanker who probably lives at home with his mum and wears her clothes when she ain't about.

I pick up Deep Purple and stick it in me pocket when the young bloke's countin some change out to a punter. I'm thinkin I better make the most of it while he's busy, and stick AC/DC in quick. All done. And they ain't got a fuckin clue. Just pick me last one up on the way out, and it's off to the next gaff.

But I'm fuckin careless. I don't like the look of the young fella, and wanna get the job done quick. When I go for The Stones I knock over a stack of fuckin Leo Sayer discount tapes. Shit. I look round. Everyone's lookin at me. Young bloke, specially. I'm weighin him up, and he's doin the same, like the O.K. fuckin Corral. I can see what I want, I'm nearly touchin it, but he won't take his fuckin eyes off me.

Fuck it. He's gotta get over the counter and through the shop before he gets to me, and I'm almost on the fuckin door as it is. Odds in me favour. I grab the tape and have it away on me toes.

I'm runnin. Fuckin peggin it. I ain't done that in a while, and pretty soon I'm fucked. All them fags, see. All them fags since I was twelve. I'm leggin it round the corner, and down this alley, and me lungs are fuckin burnin. I'm headin for Petticoat Lane cos I know I can lose the fucker there. But the cunt's still behind me, and I can hear his size tens slammin on the pavement like a fuckin machine gun.

Thommo's waitin not far off. I can see him, and he's fuckin shittin himself. He looks more fuckin scared than what I am. I'm thinkin all he's gotta do is trip this cunt up, stamp on his bollocks, and we're fuckin away. I try and shout something to him but nothing comes out cos I'm too fucked. And as I'm gettin nearer, instead of waitin for this geezer chasin me, Thommo's havin it away on his toes himself, the stupid cunt.

We're stumblin now, me and Thommo. The market's just round the corner, but we're both fucked on our feet and this cunt's still on our case. Thommo's more fucked than me, his lungs bein all stuck up with Copydex or whatever the fuck he's had up his snout lately, but I ain't fairin much better. Market ain't far, and it's gonna be packed, so we ain't got long till we can lose this cunt. Just gotta keep goin.

But there's this bloke right up ahead of us, right in our way, goin down a rubbish bin. Fuckin huge, he is. Shaved head. Wearin this big dirty green parka like a tent.

And there's something about him.

I forget about this fucker chasin me, cos I think we've lost him anyway, and I slow down. Got me hands on me knees, bent over, catchin me breath. Thommo's carried on without me, got his second wind and he's took off like his fuckin arse is on fire. And I'm watchin this bloke pull a bit of pizza out the bin.

Thommo's noticed I ain't with him.

'Fuckin come on, John! Come on!' he screams, then turns on a fuckin sixpence and carries on runnin.

And the big man turns his head to me, chewin on the pizza. His eyes are like they got too big some time, and they sort of burst out his head, and he's got these dark circles under em like he ain't had a sleep for fuckin years. And the fat's hangin off his face like a bloodhound.

He's lookin at me, straight in me eyes, but he ain't sayin a word, like he can't even see me. Like I ain't even there.

Kenny.

And I want him to say something to me. Anything. Just so I know he's in there proper, so I know he's all right. Mind you, I've just caught him goin down a fuckin bin for his dinner, so it don't look good. Then I hear them size tens bangin down the street again and I remember why I can't breathe no more.

***

The three of us is over The Barmy, me, Keith, and Thommo. Me legs are still fuckin killin me from gettin away from the fucker out the record shop. I ain't said nothing about Kenny to Keith or Thommo. We got business to discuss.

Me and Keith's on the swings, knockin back some of Thommo's old man's cheap cider, and Thommo's sprawled out on the roundabout, off his nut on a bag of glue. And there's these two little fuckers spinnin him round and round and round. He's already chucked his guts up once and it looks like these little bastards are seein if they can get another load out of him.

Keith's on his third can, and I've snapped open me fourth. He's quiet, Keith, like he's thinkin or something.

'John?'

'Yeah?'

'What you reckon on Thommo's old man?'

'His old man?'

'Yeah, I mean, you know, d'you reckon he's muggin us off?'

Muggin us off?

Keith ain't stupid. He's just bein careful. We both like Thommo, see. Like him loads. Wouldn't wanna hurt him. But course his old man's muggin us off. I mean, it's us that does the fuckin business, and it's him takes all the fuckin money. And what he weighs us out end of the week just ain't fuckin worth it no more. And after the other day, I'm ready to jack the whole fuckin thing in. I look back at Thommo on the roundabout. Don't want him to hear us. Not slaggin off his old man. No chance of that, though, not the way those little bastards are chuckin him round.

'Fuckin right he's muggin us off, Keith,' I says. 'He's been fleecin us fuckin ragged since the day we fuckin started, mate.'

Keith chucks his empty beer can in the bushes, and blows his cheeks out.

'So what you thinkin?' I says.

'We ain't kids no more, Johnny. Time we fuckin moved it up a notch.'

Keith's a steady lad. Knows what he's talkin about. And he's fuckin right. This film comes in me head, something I see when I was little. Can't shake it.

'It's like that thing,' I says to him, still tryin to think of the name of the film, 'that thing with those kids, nickin and stuff, and they give it all to that filthy old cunt with the beard.'

'Fuck me, yeah,' Keith says, 'I know what you mean. Fuck, what was it?'

There's a thud from the roundabout and the two little fuckers are runnin away, pissin themselves. Thommo's come right off. He's tryin to stand up but he's all over the fuckin place.

'Cunts!' he shouts back at em, shakin his fist. 'I'll fuckin have you next time.'

They couldn't have been more than eight or nine, but I'd still rate em against Thommo in the state he's in.

'Thommo?' I shouts. 'What's the name of that film with all them kids nickin stuff? Old. Got music in it where they all sing, and shit?'

'Fucked if I know,' he says, stumblin towards us.

'Dodger,' says Keith. 'Something Dodger.'

Then I got it.

'Fuckin Oliver Twist, ain't it. Fuckin Oliver Twist. And who was that old cunt?'

'Fagin,' Keith says, like he's just found a pot of fuckin gold.

'That's it,' I say. 'Fuckin Fagin.'

We both sit back on the swings, sort of relieved.

'What the fuck's that gotta do with anything?' Thommo says.

Gonna have to tell him. Only fair. So Keith gives it to him straight.

'It's your old man, Thommo. Me and John's thinkin of knockin it on the head.'

Thommo puts his head down a bit, like he don't wanna look at us, and puts his hands in his pockets.

'Yeah?' he says.

Me and Keith nod our heads. He's a good mate, Thommo, but his old man's a waste of fuckin space. I mean, he's got his own fuckin boy out thievin for him. His own fuckin boy.

Thommo goes and sits on the bottom of the slide and starts

chuckin bits of dirt at the roundabout.

'Have a look at this,' Keith says to me, and pulls this week's local out his back pocket.

The front page got a picture of an offie with loads of Police tape over the front.

'Been done three times last six months,' Keith says. 'And again last Friday.'

Move it up a notch. Makes fuckin sense to me.

CHAPTER EIGHTEEN

The job's set for Friday night. Thommo's been beggin us to have him along, but he's so smacked off his face half the time, Keith reckons he'll be a fuckin liability. In the end, just to shut him up, we tell him he can keep an eye out front while me and Keith go in and do the business. Thommo's promised he won't stick nothing up his snout for a couple of days before, but I don't believe a fuckin word of that.

The offie's up the end of the Mile End Road, near Stepney Green Station. Keith reckons we can get the job done in five minutes, hop on a train, and be back in bed for cocoa and crumpets before you can say Jack fuckin Robinson.

***

Couple weeks beforehand, me and Keith goes in to case the joint, check out the lay of the land. We get out at Stepney Green, and the gaff's right on top of us.

It's just your normal offie. Stacks of beer in pyramids, wall to wall bottles, couple of birds, mid-fifties, behind the counter, till apiece. One of em looks a bit rough, like she'd stripe you soon as look at you, but the other one looks all right. There's a back room through a curtain, but it's shut and we can't see in. Probably just a little tea-room or something. No wonder the gaff's been done over so fuckin much. Fuckin askin for it with this set-up.

We don't wanna hurt no one, specially not a couple of birds old enough to be our mums, but if push comes to shove, you know, job's gotta get done proper. You can't be too fuckin careful in this game.

***

So, Friday night comes round, and it's fuckin pissin down. A couple of minutes out of Stepney Green, we're soaked to the fuckin skin. Turns out to be a bit of a touch though, the rain sheetin down like this, cos there ain't no bastard about. We come to the row of shops where the offie is. I look at me watch. Five minutes to closin. Bang on the dot. Everything other than the kebab shop and the offie are shuttered up. Wind's gettin up and the rain's comin right into our faces. Fuckin weather.

'You ready for this, John?' Keith says.

I'm fuckin ready. Never felt more ready in me whole fuckin life.

Thommo parks himself one side of the door.

'I'll just hang about here then, you know, watch out for Old Bill,' he says, and we leave him there. He seems a bit jumpy to me. Bit too fuckin keen. Dunno whether it's his nerves or he's had a sneaky fuckin snifter of something when we weren't lookin.

I'm feelin fuckin fantastic. More alive than I felt me whole fuckin life.

Keith checks again if I'm all right.

'Yeah, mate. You?'

Keith nods, the way he does sometimes when you know he's thinkin about something but ain't quite worked out how it's makin him feel. Thommo's yackin away, talkin absolute fuckin bollocks. He better be clean. He better be fuckin clean.

Here we go.

Keith's in first. Little bell rings on the door. He goes left, I go right. And we both see it at the same time – a fuckin metal grill thing all the way round the fuckin counter right up to the ceilin, just a gap at the front to slip the booze through and take the money, and a flip top to go in and out one side. Fuck. Never expected a fuckin metal grill thing. Don't reckon Keith did neither. But he ain't showin it. It's me what's shittin it. I ain't got a fuckin clue what to do. Must have had it put up since last time we was in. Same two birds, though. The one with the front's clocked the look on our faces, and you can tell she's ready for a fuckin tear-up. Got a smile on her like someone's cut it into her face with a Stanley knife. The other one's comin out the little room out the back just as we come in the shop.

'Can I help you, love?

It's the lairy one. She's talkin to Keith. She knows we ain't on the fuckin level and we gotta go. And we gotta fuckin go. But Keith, he's goin up to the counter and he's fetchin something out his coat. Fuckin hell, he never said nothing about no shooters. I'm shittin myself, now, really fuckin shittin it. But it's only his wallet, and he picks up three beers. Me face is givin it away all over the gaff, and that hard bitch has gotta be pissin herself.

Keith pays for the beers and we turn round to go, then . . .

CRASH

Thommo's burst in through the fuckin door, all balaclavered up.

For fuck's sake.

'GIVE US THE FUCKIN' MONEY!' he screams. Off his nut, obviously. He tries to jump the counter but he don't know about the fuckin metal grill thing, can't even fuckin see it the state he's in. And he bounces straight off. Stupid bastard's sparko by the counter.

I dunno what to do, but Keith's got this look on him like this ain't over. Right calm, he puts two of the bottles on the floor then breaks the other one on a shelf. Then he walks up to the side of the counter, frontin the hard bitch.

'The man said, give us the fuckin money,' he says, cold, you know, like Clint Eastwood.

The other bird's took off out the back soon as Thommo smashed into the screen, but the one Keith's frontin up, fuck, she's broke a bottle for herself and she's wavin it about in Keith's face like she's done this sort of thing a million fuckin times.

'Come on then, you little fucker.' she says. 'Fuckin come on then'

I'm fuckin froze. It's all gone fuckin pear-shaped and I can't think. I got two mates in the whole fuckin world. One's knocked himself out on a fuckin metal grill thing, and the other one's about to get bottled by a granny. I feel for the penknife in me pocket. Never go nowhere without it. Habit. I know the Old Bill's comin in a minute, cos the other bird must've rung em by now. And all I'm seein's Thommo sparko on the floor and this old girl wavin a broken bottle in Keith's face. And I fuckin lose it. I jump over Thommo, knockin over a stack of beers on the way, and stand side to side with Keith. I get me blade right close in her face. I can see it's rattled her. She's hard, fuck me, she is, but this is two geezers frontin her now, and she ain't havin none of that. She lets Keith past. But while Keith's unloadin the till, she takes a swing at the back of his head with the bottle.

Can't have that. And when the Old Bill crash in, I've got her by the hair and the blade at her throat. Keith's fuckin red-handed, stuffin the cash in his coat. There's six of em, Old Bill, that is.

'Put the fuckin blade down, son. Put the blade down.'

And I'm lookin at them, and they're lookin at me, and I'm lookin at this bird. Her eyes have all softened up, like she wants out. And I might as well be lookin at me own mum, you know, or me nan. Then she changes again. It's in her eyes, that's where I see it first. She ain't cocky no more, or even soft. She's just fuckin terrified. And, for a moment, in them eyes, I see Kenny and his old girl and how they looked when the old man was tearin into em that time I was over for tea. And a million other times, I should fuckin reckon.

And this old girl's eyes, they look like that. But it ain't Kenny's old man she's scared of. It's me. And I dunno why she's lookin at me like that, like she thinks I'm really gonna hurt her or something.

I lower the blade a bit.

'Look,' I says. 'Look, shit, we didn't mean nothing, you know, we didn't wanna hurt no one. We just, look, fuckin, sorry. All right? Sorry.'

And I fuckin am. I know I am. I can feel the tears burnin in me eyes.

'Son, put it down.'

The Old Bill are gettin nearer. Edgin closer. I can see Keith out the corner of me eye. He's got his hands up, cos there ain't nothin else he can do, and he's starin at em like he's some sort of fuckin nutter. Then I see two of the Old Bill grab hold of Thommo and start draggin him out. And that's it for me. It's just like Kenny all over, that time in the playground. And I go again. I drop the old girl and go for the nearest copper. I can feel Keith behind me, and I know he's thinkin the same. Side by side. To the fuckin end. But this ain't school no more, this is real fuckin life. And we're on the ground in seconds, hands up our backs, gettin dragged out the shop in the rain.

***

They had us on remand in separate J.D.C.s - Juvenile Detention Centres. Thatcher shut down the Borstals proper about the time Kenny got banged up, but it's the same shit, just a different name. While I'm here, I get used to just shuttin me eyes to it all. Don' t wanna think about nothing no more. By the time our case comes up, I can't hardly remember what I done.

And there weren't never gonna be no fuckin sympathy for the likes of us. Judge would've fuckin had us hung from the nearest fuckin lamp-post, if he'd had his way. In the end, he might as well of done.

Keith holds his hands up to bein behind the whole fuckin job. Says he twisted me and Thommo's arms to help him out. I tell the judge it weren't fuckin true, told him I was in it all the way.

All three of us is in the dock at the end. Keith's starin straight at the beak, same way like when I first see him in class all them years back. Me, I'm shittin myself, but I'm starin at the beak like Keith best I can. And it's easier than what I thought cos I don't even feel sorry for what I done or nothing. The whole world's gone all too fuckin dark for that.

I can't look at Mum, though, so I'm sort of just lookin at the floor most of the time, other than when I'm starin the beak down. But Thommo, poor old Thommo, he's fuckin lost it. Dunno if it's the glue all them years what's done it, or what, but he's jabberin to himself, all quiet, teeth all gritted, foamin at the sides of his mouth. Shakin all over, he is. And every now and then he'll shout out 'CUNTS.' then go back to his jabberin. Second time he does it, Judge has him took straight out.

Judge said me and Keith weren't nothing but a couple of cold-hearted thugs. Give us six year apiece. J.D.C. till we're twenty-one, then the rest in the big nick. Neither one of us bats a fuckin eyelid. And Thommo, poor fuckin Thommo, he gets fuckin sectioned. Another one for the nut-house. Judge seemed proper fuckin sad for him, though. So was I. Poor bastard.

Mum comes and sees me in the cells under the court before they take me away, Mum and Uncle Derek. She's sittin on the bed next to me, and Uncle Derek's leanin up against the bars, his arms folded, lookin at the floor. I can't look at neither fuckin one of em much, specially not that cunt. Dunno what the fuck he's doin here, anyway. Or Mum. I mean, she ain't sayin nothing, just fuckin cryin. Like I fuckin need that, don't I. Cryin really soft, she is, like you can't hardly hear her.

Then I close me eyes till everything's black, and her cryin's the only sound I can hear.

**

When the Old Bill comes to take me away, Mum stays sittin on the bed. She don't move a muscle. Don't even turn round and see me out. And when I go past Uncle Derek, I'm about to give him a piece of me fuckin mind, you know, leave him with something to really fuckin chew on, when I see he's got tears runnin down his face, and he's shakin like a leaf.

Something moves inside me, makes me wanna throw up, and I can't walk.

'It's all right, son,' says one of the coppers. 'Take your time.'

Uncle Derek looks at me, puts a hand on me shoulder and holds it round the back of me neck. Puts his forehead on mine. Just holds it there. He ain't sayin a word. Don't have to. That touch, the tears in his eyes, it's all fuckin too much. And there's Mum, sittin on the bed, still not bearin to look at me. I wanna say sorry. I wanna get down on me knees and tell em from me heart how sorry I am, but I know it'd fuckin rip me in half to do it.

The copper tugs me arm a bit, meanin for me to go.

'Come on, son,' he says.

Uncle Derek takes his hand from me neck and rubs it backwards through his hair, and sits down on the bed next to Mum, a broken fuckin man.

I close me eyes as the copper's takin me away, and all I can hear are his footsteps marchin down the corridor and Elvis bangin in me head.

CHAPTER NINETEEN

I'm in the Old Bill van, comin away from the court, on me way to the J.D.C. in Wandsworth nick. There's me and half a dozen other lads, all givin it the bigg'un, sizin each other up, tryin to make out we ain't fuckin shittin ourselves. Dunno about them, but I'm fuckin cackin it. Had it in me head to play it like Ray Winstone in 'Scum' but lookin round at these lads, I know that's a non-fuckin-starter. Half of em's got eyes like Kenny, which fuckin freaks me out, and the other cunts, they're three times me fuckin size.

I'm way out me depth here. Fuckin know it. Deep breath. Keep me head down, me nose clean, and do me bird like a good little boy, and with a bit of luck, I'll be out in three.

Dunno where they've sent Thommo or Keith. Last time I see Keith was when the beak sent us down, and last time I see Thommo he was bein dragged out of court by his toes, screamin, callin everyone a cunt.

***

I get the piss ripped out of me soon as I get in the nick. Screws must've put the word out beforehand, and I'm down as Sissy Sissons the Granny-Basher. They're all at me. Screws, lags, fuckin everyone.

But as it goes, days ain't bad in here, after a while. Not much different from when I was at school. We got our jobs, you know, gardenin, kitchens, cleanin, that sort of shit. Like I says, it's all right. Every day's the fuckin same, though, which does your head in sometimes, but fair's fair, I had it comin.

Mum's here every week, bang on the dot. Brings me bits what I need, you know, whatever I tell her. Won't bring no snouts, though, not for all the fuckin askin. Tells me bits of news, mostly what I don't give a fuck about, other than I was fuckin gutted when she said Old Cartwright pegged it. Scared the fuck out of me as a kid, he did, but I'll never forget him at Dad's funeral, tears in his big, scratched-up eyes, army medals hangin off his chest. Sort of would've liked to have known him better, if you know what I mean, if I had me time over.

Mad Mrs Jessup passed not long after, and Mum says the Council's moved these Indian families straight in, both sides. Reckons they're nice people an all, but me and her both know the old street ain't never gonna be the same.

First few visits, Mum's got Becky with her. And all the while, in that noisy, filthy visiting room, the whole time she's there, all Becky does is sit there readin her book like she ain't got a care in the fuckin world. Mum's talkin to me but I'm lookin at Becky cos I miss her so fuckin much.

Even when one of the lads kicks off, or one of the mums or dads goes garrity or something, Becky don't take no notice. And at the end, when the bell goes, she just shuts her book, holds Mum's hand, and looks at the floor. Won't look at me, let alone say anything. It's even so Mum's gotta tell her to say goodbye.

Starts me thinkin. And first time Mum comes on her own, hits me Becky never wanted to come here in the first place. And that really fuckin hurts. But you can't get into that sort of shit in here. Not in here. Gotta shut down. Do your fuckin bird and move on.

But the nights, they're the worst. Ain't nothing like a night in here. That's when the words come in your head and the faces and the missin and the heartbreak. And we all turn from fuckin effin, blindin hard bastards into little fuckin kids what just want their mums. Always someone cryin in the the dark, snifflin, you know. And age and size don't make no fuckin difference.

But it ain't never me. Not no more. You ain't got time for that shit. Can't let it drag you down. Cos tears, tears don't get you fuckin nowhere. But sometimes I lie awake at night and I can't see nothing but black and it feels like me whole body's breakin into tiny, little pieces and that if I don't cry soon I'll fuckin start drownin.

There's fights all the time. Bound to be in a place like this, but the screws crack down hard as you like. You only get caught scrappin once, if you can fuckin help it, but it don't stop some of em. Get beat black and blue by each other and black and blue by the screws. Gotta be fuckin mad. Me, I stay well fuckin clear. I don't want no trouble.

They move me to Wandsworh proper on me twenty-first, just like they promised. Mum come in with a birthday card. Footballer on the front. Fifteen nicker inside. 'Love, Mum.' I give her the card back and keep the dough for snouts. Can't hardly bear lookin at her. Every time she comes she tries to put a brave face on it, you know, tries to make it like it's just me and her at the kitchen table at home, havin a cuppa. I wish she'd just fuckin let rip sometimes, like Dad would or Uncle Derek, you know, really fuckin tear into me. All this 'love' bollocks, can't fuckin put up with much more of that.

***

I'm on 'C' wing first night in the big nick. That's where they put you before they sort you out proper. Next day, I'm shifted to 'A' wing, with the Lifers and the Remandos, and whatever poor fuckers like me they choose to send there for no fuckin reason at all.

Whole place is massive. They got five floors just on this wing, and you can't fuckin move for lags and screws.

I'm sharin a cell on the third floor, with two Remandos – Billy and Adie – and a broken shit-house. At night, there's cockroaches and fuck knows what scrabblin about. Billy and Adie's all right. Harmless enough. In here, anyway. Outside's a different fuckin matter.

Billy, he's a big bastard. Forties, skinhead, tattoos. Banged up for nearly toppin his ex's new bloke with a baseball bat. Adie, he don't say fuck all, but Billy says he's in for letter-bombin McDonald's after they give him a Big Mac instead of a Veggie Burger. Bein all coked up, Adie says he didn't notice till he's ate the whole fuckin lot. Weren't till he found the Big Mac box in his motor and the burger sick down his shirt next mornin, that he guessed what happened. And, as you do, thought he'd get the bastards back by blowin the livin shit out of em.

We get exercise twenty minutes a day in the yard. And there's a few jobs what you gotta do, but other than that, it's just keepin your nose clean.

The screws are fuckin hardcore, and even the Lifers keep their heads down. I get me first dose second night on 'A' Wing. Adie's asleep, and me and Billy's talkin about the Hammers. I try not to think about Dad, but it's so fuckin hard, you know, and I wanna cry. Bite the inside of me lip, like I always do, and everything goes away for a while. Billy reckons he's in the I.C.F. and was on the ferry in seventy-eight fightin the Mancs. Fuckin believe it an all. Hard as they fuckin come, Billy.

So, we're havin a good old natter, me and Billy, when these two screws come bargin in. Both fuckin huge. One of em tells Billy to fuck off, and the other one drags Adie out the top bunk and throws him clean out the cell. Adie and Billy take off so fuckin quick I don't see em for fuckin dust. One might be hard and the other might be mental, but they both know the fuckin score in here.

One of the screws keeps a look out while the other one picks me up by the throat and slams me up the back of the cell.

'You know what's comin to you, Sissons?' he says, so calm it's like he's teachin a class of little kids. 'You know what's fuckin comin?'

I ain't got a bleedin clue what he's talkin about but I got a fair fuckin idea what's comin. I'm thinkin it's some sort of initiation bollocks all the new lags get, you know, sort of scare the shit of you, let you know who's on top. But then this bastard, this fuckin bastard, calm as you like, pulls his head back and nuts me right in the fuckin face. Feels like I'm all caved in and I got blood and snot comin out everywhere.

'And that's just for fuckin starters,' he says, straightenin up his tie.

Then he leans down to where I'm in a fuckin heap on the floor. His face is all red and his eyes are fuckin burnin. I can tell he's lost it now, and he's growlin more than talkin. He grabs me by me hair and brings his face right in on mine. His breath fuckin reeks and he's breathin out his nose like a bull.

'I been waitin four fuckin years for you, Sissons,' he says. 'Four fuckin years.'

But his voice is just a fuckin echo.

'Think you can try and fuckin stripe my big sister and fuckin get away with it, do you? Cunt.'

And I'm thinking, shit. What are the fuckin chances of that?

Then the fucker gobs in me face and kicks me in the bollocks so fuckin hard I'm nearly passin out.

'Every fuckin day, Sissons, I'm after you,' he says, walkin out backwards, stickin his fat fuckin finger at me. 'Every fuckin day.'

Gettin up next mornin, I'm feelin something changin in me. Shiftin. Dyin. Feel it most in me eyes. It's like they're stuck open and gone too wide or something, like they're stuck in concrete.

And there's this cold air what hurts and blows through em all the fuckin time.

CHAPTER TWENTY

And that cunt what caved my face in the first night, he weren't wrong. Name's George Johnson. All the lags hate him. Proper psycho. Whenever he's about, him and his gorilla mate kick the shit right out of me. Not just me, goes on all over the gaff. At night, over the sound of the cockroaches scurryin, and Adie snorin, and Billy talkin to himself, there's these muffled screams and thuds and there's blokes in the breakfast queue in the mornin battered to fuck, and no one sayin a fuckin word.

Never fight back. That's the rule. That's what they want you to do. Me, I just stand there, eyes wide. And I take it all. And I don't feel none of it. Fight back and they'll have you in the Segregation Wing soon as fuckin look at you. No bastard hears you scream in there. But that ain't why I don't fight. I don't fight cos the standin still's the only thing holdin me together.

Three months this goes on. And every time they come in, I crawl in me dark place and stay there till it's over. Safe. Untouchable. Pain's pain, see. And when you been hurt like I have, when you see your own fuckin Dad die in front of you, and when you know you've let everyone down who ever loved you, and you know there ain't no way of comin back, well, nothing touches that. Fuckin nothing.

But that's me one mistake, see. The holdin it in. Cunts like Johnson, they wanna see you suffer, they wanna hear you beggin for your fuckin life. They ain't content with the blood and the poundin. They wanna know you're hurtin inside and out. And if you don't give em that, they'll just keep on till you fuckin hand it to em on a fuckin plate.

***

Was only a matter of time in the end. Just a matter of time. Johnson's off all week, then he's on nights, so I'm all right for a few days. I know his shifts back to front. Make it my business, you know, cos then I can set me mind when I get up, set it for whatever's comin.

Adie's still asleep, and me and Billy's talkin about what a fuckin scandal it was Pop Robson never played for England, when the cell door opens.

Two screws. Never seen em before. Skinny bastards, and their eyes are gleamin and they're grinnin like a couple of kids just broke into a fuckin sweet shop. Me and Billy's lookin at each other. The both of us know these two cunts have come to play.

'Right you two,' one of em says, talkin to Billy and Adie, even though Adie's still asleep, 'fuck off out of here.'

But I ain't takin it off these scrawny fucks. No fuckin way. Johnson, fair enough, I mean if someone did that to my Becky, I'd probably be the fuckin same. But not these two. They ain't got the fuckin right. Billy knows it an all, and he ain't movin.

The two screws move in. One of em goes over to Adie and tries draggin him out of bed. The other one comes over to Billy. Gets right in his face. Billy looks at me, winks, and stands up. And as he reaches the height of this little screw, he nuts him right in the face and walks out the cell.

The other screw's still tryin to drag Adie out of bed, but Adie ain't havin none of it. Must be holdin on to the fuckin sides or something. Mind you, we've all been doin that for years.

And that does it for me. Like I says, they ain't got the fuckin right. The screw with his face mashed in, he's out of it, can't hardly stand up. But I'm on him anyway. I got me arm across his throat, smashin me fist into his ribs. And I keep poundin till I feel one crack. And another. And another.

I've really fuckin lost it now, dunno what the fuck I'm doin. It's like all that darkness inside's comin out all at once, all on this cunt. And I can't fuckin stop.

Don't take long till the other cunt's leggin it out the cell, tryin to blow his whistle. But I know there ain't no one comin. They fucked up, see. This is Johnson's business and no other screw's gonna fuck with him.

Billy and Adie's shifted out to another cell that afternoon. Don't take a fuckin genius to know what I got comin.

***

But I can't do it no more. The standin still. You can only do that sort of shit so long before something goes. Something deep. It's like all the world outside – Mum, Becks, all of em – none of em matter no more. Cos all I got in me head's this cunt Johnson, and how I'm gonna have him out of here in a box. Dunno how I'm gonna do it yet. Fuckin no idea. But I gotta start fightin back before it's me dragged out this shit-hole by me feet.

Next day, I'm in the wood shop, and I get this idea. Ain't no way I'm walkin out here with a Stanley blade or a fuckin claw hammer, they're all tagged. So I pick myself up a couple of nails and slip em in me socks.

Back in me cell, I'll knock me up a little something. Slip the nails between me fingers, tear off a bit of sheet and strap me hand up, like a boxer, and push the nails through. Bob's your uncle, a tasty little knuckle-duster. I'm closin me eyes, and I can feel the nails goin in through that bastard's throat and I'm grindin em in and his blood's splattin me face but I don't care a fuck. And I'm gonna make him look at me as I'm rippin his throat out, make sure I'm the last person he ever fuckin sees. I don't care no more what happens, long as I can see that look in his eyes. Fear and panic and fuckin death.

***

I'm still in a right fuckin state from the last beatin I got from Johnson, when out the blue I hears a voice from the past.

'Fuck me, Johnny Sissons!'

A slimy, greasy sort of voice. The sort that'll promise you the earth and give you fuck all in return.

Long time since I heard someone halfway friendly, though. Ain't fuckin seen hide nor hair of Adie and Billy since they was shifted. Reckon they're gettin it right bad somewhere. But there's only one rule in here, one rule that wipes out all the others. And that rule is simple: 'Look out for your fuckin self'.

So I hears this voice. Not that it's friendly, like I says. More, familiar. Terry Wilkins. Terry fuckin Wilkins. Harry Wilkins' slitherin shit of a big brother. He's runnin down the steps from the landin above, two at a time and I meet him halfway down. He steps back when he sees the state I'm in.

'Fuckin hell, Johnny. What happened to you?'

He's talkin like he's me best mate or something. Like he really fuckin cares. Gives me the fuckin creeps, he does. But it's a face I know, and that's something after what I been through.

I give him the old line.

'Fell down the stairs.'

He looks at me like he's really fuckin concerned, you know, genuine, like. But I know him. Born arse-licker. Always fuckin was.

'Hear you went down for the Granny job,' he says, as we're

walkin along.

Ain't got the energy to tell him she weren't no older than me mum, so I let it slide.

Seems a fuckin lifetime ago. Anyway, what the fuck's he want me to say? He knows why I'm here.

'What you in for?' I says. Not that I'm really fuckin bothered.

'Ah, just some shit, you know, Johnny. Be out in six months.'

He puts his arm round me. I wanna tell him to fuck off, but all this pushin people away fuckin takes it out of you in the end.

'Look, Johnny. Whatever grief you're gettin in here, I can get it sorted.'

He's pretendin he don't know nothing about it, about Johnson. But cunts like Terry Wilkins make it their business to know every fuckin thing from here to fuckin bedtime.

Same as at school. Always had his ear to the ground and his nose where it shouldn't. Reckoned he could get you anything an all. Football stickers, chocolate, fags, chocolate fags if you want em. Fuckin anything. Never come through though. Always some bleedin story, like he's had a rush on, or Jacko's nabbed his stash, or his fence has turned him over, you know, some such bollocks. Far as I know, no one ever saw fuck all. That's Terry Wilkins for you. All fuckin talk.

Still, might as well humour the cunt. Got fuck all else to do. 'What do you mean, "sorted"?' I says.

'I got . . . connections, mate. You know? People.'

Here we go. Same old fuckin bollocks. I tell him I can sort me own shit out, but thanks anyway. He knows I don't believe a word he's fuckin sayin.

'No, really, Johnny, I'm . . . there's this bloke I work for. He's proper fuckin kosher, John, you know? The real fuckin deal. He can really fuckin help you out, mate.'

I just wanna be on me own now. Had enough of this cunt.

'Remember you was pretty quick with your hands as a kid, Johnny. Always thought I'd end up seein you at the York Hall one of these days. Still got the old one-two?' And he throws a couple of jabs as he says it.

Scrap I had with them two screws was the first I had in years, not since I first got in the J.D.C., But I know I ain't lost it. I can see it in their faces – the other lags. I know they think I'm a right proper headcase. But what I lost is the fire. The focus, you know. That's what I lost.

Till I had this idea of rippin George Johnson's fuckin throat out.

And I dunno why I'm even talkin to this cunt, of all fuckin people. Always was a tosser. Just like his little shit of a brother. Terry blows out his cheeks and walks away scratchin his chin, like he's makin a show of makin his mind up about something. Thinks it makes him look like he's got some sort of fuckin influence in the matter, you know.

'You ever heard of Ronnie Swordfish?' he says, turnin round.

Now what sort of a fuckin name is that? I'm thinkin he's probably made it up on the fuckin spot. But he's dead serious, and I tighten me face up.

'Course,' he says, 'you been out the scene a while, John. Forgot that.'

Scene? What fuckin scene? Cunt thinks he's in the fuckin Godfather.

He pulls me to one side as we're makin our way to the next landin. Starts talkin really low so I can't hardly hear him.

'Ronnie's been round for fuckin ages, mate. Got the whole fuckin manor sewed up. Thing is, John, we got a couple lads inside, you know, long term bird. We could do with a geezer like you on the Firm. I can put in a good word for Ronnie, if you're interested?'

He's really gettin on me fuckin nerves now. All this gangster shit.

'Told you, Terry,' I says, shruggin his arm off me shoulder. 'I'm sortin this out myself.'

* * *

I forget about Terry Wilkins soon as I'm back in me cell. Johnson ain't back for a couple of days, so I'm lookin forward to gettin me head down for a bit, but I got two screws outside me cell the whole fuckin time. It's like they're keepin an eye on me special or something. And it ain't never been like that before. That night, Johnson comes in mob-handed a day fuckin early.

Some cunt's tipped him off, and him and three other fuckers rip into me till they can't hardly fuckin stand up. Gets so bad, I start passin out, but every time I do, when it starts goin black and feels like I'm fallin, one of em slaps me in the face till I wake up and they start on me again. In the end, when me eyes are closin over and I can't even feel any fuckin part of me, they fuck off. George Johnson says something to me before he goes, but he can't hardly fuckin breathe he's so fucked, and I don't get a fuckin word of it. When he's finished sayin whatever it is he's sayin, I lean back against the wall and let myself go.

And I'm floatin and sinkin and swirlin and meltin. The black's movin round me and through me and I don't know where I stop and the outside starts. I'm spinnin round and round and round and in and out and deep, so deep. I'm sinkin into meself, right into nowhere, to the place where nothing ever stops.

I'm in a room. It's dark. But there's a light. And there's a boy sittin on a bed. He's got his head bent and he ain't seen me yet. I've been here before. This room. This dark. A long time ago. There's a sadness and there's a hurt in this room and so many tears. I'm standin up and I'm walkin round, and still he don't look up. There's nothing here but so much fuckin pain. It's like I gotta tear through it all just to put one foot in front of another. I'm lookin for something but the light outside the window starts buzzin, and goes out. Flicker. Flicker. Out. On again. And it's Kenny's room. But it ain't Kenny on the bed. It's me. Lookin at the light. The light outside his window.

'Mr Sissons? Mr Sissons?'

The light gets bigger till that's all there is. And the back of me eyes are fuckin killin me.

'What?'

Fuck me. Never felt so much fuckin pain. Feels like me head's in a fuckin vice and I got ten geezers stampin on me bollocks.

'Thought we'd lost you there, Mr Sissons. For a moment.'

I'd been in the prison hospital three fuckin weeks and didn't know fuck all about it. One of the five ribs George Johnson and his fuckin mates done went straight through one of me lungs. Doctor reckons I was lucky to make it through the first night. Said that'd teach me for assaultin a warder. Assaultin a fuckin warder. Bastards. Story goes I jumped Johnson when he popped his head round to say hello, and I tried to rip his fuckin eyes out with me fingers. Said it took six screws to pull me off the cunt.

***

I'm headin up the steps to me landin when me collar gets felt. Fuck me. Ain't been out more than fuckin twenty minutes.

'Governor wants to see you, Sissons.' The screw spits the words out like I make him fuckin sick just to look at.

And every screw I pass is lookin just the fuckin same.

***

Governor's office is wood all over. Big fuck-off desk, all panelled walls. Half a fuckin library behind this glass case. He stands up when I come in. Little bloke. Face like a beetroot. Ain't hard to tell he's fuckin steamin. The two screws what brought me here ain't said a word since they come and got me. Something's up. Fuckin know that.

'Sit down, Sissons,' the Governor says, and stays standin, just like that cunt Jacko used to at school before he caned your fuckin arse off.

I sit down and the two screws move in behind me.

Governor puts his hands on the desk and leans into me face. I fuckin ain't havin this. I've had too many years of this shit. No more Mister fuckin Nice Guy.

I try and stand up but the two screws push me straight back down.

'What?' I says. 'What d'you fuckin want?'

Governor smacks me round the face and the two screws hold me in the chair, bendin me arms back and pushin me forward so me head goes down.

'Let him up, lads.'

Bastards let me up, but they ain't lettin go. The Governor shoves a newspaper under me nose. Big headlines.

'Car Bomb Outside South London School'

I keep readin.

Yesterday afternoon, a car bomb exploded outside Wandsworth Junior and Infants school on Church Road, killing two adults and a child. The victims were named as Mr George Johnson (45), his wife Angela (37), and their five year old daughter, Lilly.'

Can't read no more.

And the blood's poolin in me shoe where the nails are diggin in me foot.

***

First lag I see when I come out the Governor's Office is Terry Wilkins. Smilin. Goes to shake me hand.

I bang the cunt right in the face.

He's lookin up at me from the floor, like he dunno why I done it. Like blowin up a little fuckin five year old ain't enough. I ain't got nothing more to say to this cunt.

***

Screws leave me alone for the rest of me bird, mostly. Terry Wilkins is never far from a fuckin screw at all fuckin times and a couple months later he's on his way. Good fuckin behaviour, would you fuckin Adam 'n' Eve it. I get meself a bit of a name inside with the lags. When I'm up for me first parole, they turn me down. Always gonna fuckin happen. The Old Bill had a word when Johnson got done, but they couldn't prove nothing cos I was fuckin inside when it happened, but every bastard in here thinks I done him in. Him and his family. There ain't no fuckin changin that. I don't feel bad about Johnson. He was a cunt. He had it comin. But his missus. Fuck. And his little girl. I mean, for fuck's sake. Five years old.

Can't sleep for thinkin of Becky when she was that age. So funny, she was. Just learnin, you know, just startin out. Learnin with her laughin and her gigglin and she was so fuckin lovely. There's tears in me eyes most nights but I can't let em go. Cos if I do, I won't never stop. And I know I owe Ronnie Swordfish big time for gettin rid of Johnson. Fuckin big time. But all I can think of is that little girl. Five fuckin years old. And it feels like I killed her me fuckin self, even though I never. I got her blood on me hands, and no amount of fuckin scrubbin's gettin it off.

Me parole date keeps gettin put back cos the Governor thinks it's funny to start makin up shit about me. Ends up, the bastards stick nearly two fuckin years on me sentence. But then a different Governor comes along. Young geezer. All fuckin holier than thou, but a nice bloke. Knows his stuff. And that's me on me way.

Seven years. Seven fuckin years.

***

Mum's last visit before they let me out, she tells me Kenny's old girl got pulled dead out the water at Southwark Bridge.

CHAPTER TWENTY-ONE

Mum comes runnin across the road soon as she sees me, high heels clatterin, face all painted up. Fuck me, she looks a million dollars. I can't hardly hold me head up to front her. Feel so weak, you know, like the life's just fell out of me. She's got this nice coat on, some sort of snide fur, and she puts her arms round me and holds me to her and she feels so soft, and there's me, feelin about four fuckin years old and all I wanna do is I just stay here in her arms.

A white van comes up the road. Slows down and pulls up at the kerb. Charlie Paynter. What the fuck's he doin here? He leans over and winds down the window.

'All right, John?' he says, half an eye on Mum.

I've tensed up. Mum can feel it. She turns her head round to him, and pulls back from me a bit, then looks me dead in the face, like she's tryin to say something just by the doin of it.

Fuck. Never thought about that. Never thought Mum . . .

Dad.

Mum says Charlie's takin us home, and says about me gettin in the van.

She gets in the van, and moves up close to him, leavin room for me.

'Come on, John,' she says.

I wanna tell her I'll make me own way, but I never been south of the Water till they shipped me here seven year back, and the way me head is right now I dunno how the fuck I'd get myself home. And that's the only place I wanna be right now. Home. With Becky. Thinkin of her makes me mind up and I jump in the front with Mum and Charlie.

We're sittin in the van all squashed up, and no one sayin a word. I'm lookin out me window at places I ain't never seen before and I can feel Mum lookin at me the whole time. She's got her hand on me leg and I know she wants me to say something, anything, but I ain't got nothing to say. Not to her.

Don't even wanna fuckin look at her.

Crossin the River, I know I'm comin home. And as we're goin through Shoreditch, me heart's fuckin poundin. Canning Town,

Bow, Plaistow, Bethnal Green, Custom House, all the East End, all of it's a fuckin shit-hole, but it runs in me blood, see, and bein here again's like seein a mountain for the first time, or the sea, or something like that. Sort of overwhelming, you know. Not that I seen no fuckin seas or mountains, but I reckon if I did, if I ever did, this is what it'd feel like.

I tell Charlie to drop me outside The Barmy and I go in the playground. Sit on the swings. Place is empty and it's like I can feel Keith sittin next to me, tellin me everything's gonna be all right and the wind's blowin the roundabout round and round and round like it ain't never gonna stop. And it's cold. So fuckin cold. Could sit here for fuckin ever, thinkin about Keith and Thommo, thinkin about how it used to be. But knowin where they are now just makes me feel so fuckin sad. I asked Mum about em every time she come to visit, you know, if she'd heard anything. She said Thommo's old man had disappeared off the face of the earth, so she don't know about him, and Keith's family don't even talk to her. Blamin it on me, see, their boy bein banged up. That cunt Johnson told me once he'd heard Keith was bein a right fucker up north. Told me he won't see the light of day for fuckin years. Laughin when he said it. Bastard.

Can't take much more of sittin here and I'm soon on me way home.

And as I'm walkin these streets, breathin in the car fumes, skippin round the dog shit, it's like nothing's changed. Not on the front, anyways. But there's a different feel to the place. And pretty soon I start openin me eyes to it all. Shops, what people's wearin, music comin out of houses and cars. It's all different, like they all carried on without me. Left me behind. And I feel sort of see-through, and it's like everyone's lookin at me and I'm disappearin with every fuckin step.

I go past me old school. Isaac Meade. Playtime. Hundreds of kids runnin round, not a care in the fuckin world. There's some lads playin football just where we used to, up the top by the road. And you can tell on their faces kickin that tennis ball about's all they ever wanna fuckin do for the rest of their little lives. I stop awhile, and watch.

And there's this kid, looks a bit like me when I was that age. Better than the others by a fuckin mile, he is. And he's past one, then another and he's gonna shoot, when this fat kid comes out of fuckin nowhere and kicks him up in the air. Cuts him right in fuckin half, he does. And that starts a big fuckin free for all, twenty kids pilin into each other. The kid what got fouled, he's turned into a fuckin animal, swingin and swearin and beatin the shit out of whoever's fuckin nearest. I gotta walk away at this point. Can't fuckin stand it.

It's pissin down now, and the wind's blowin me off the street.

I'm half thinkin of goin over Keith's, seein his mum and dad, you know, but I feel so fuckin tired. I'll do it tomorrow. Only right I see em. Nice people. Never forget his mum faintin fuckin dead away when Keith got sent down, and his dad just holdin her like she was gonna break into a million pieces. Just thinkin of em like that makes me a bit, you know, a bit fuckin wary of seein em again. Specially with em blankin Mum an that.

I'm turnin the corner down our street. Charlie's van's pullin up outside our house. Must've stopped off on the way. Mum could never go fuckin nowhere without pickin something up. Used to drive Dad mad. Her and Charlie's talkin, and she's give him a peck on the cheek. Then she gets out and Charlie drives off real slow. I'm walkin waist deep in shit now, and every step's takin me further away. Mum's waitin at the front gate. And I gets this big lump in me throat. Can't fuckin swallow it for the fuckin life of me, and it sort of stops me breath for a second and I gets this feelin I wanna run somewhere, run away from the whole fuckin lot of em just so I can be on me own for a while.

I look across the street at Kenny's house so I don't have to look at Mum. All the lights are off, and next door, where he used to live, where his old man topped himself, it's still all boarded up.

Then I see the lights are off in our house an all. And the curtains are shut. Thought Becky might be watchin for me, you know. But she ain't.

Mum smiles weak and sort of awkward when I come near, and her eyes are all filled up. I wanna ask her where Becky is, thinkin she might be over one of me Aunties' or something, but then it hits me: Becky's gonna be sixteen next month and she don't need no lookin after no more. Fuckin sixteen years old. My little Becky.

When we go in the house, Mum switches on the light in the hall. And there's this new carpet goin all the way up the stairs. I'm thinkin Mum's had a touch at the shop, you know, moved up a bit, or Becky's got herself a little part-time job, but then I settle it's probably Charlie's helpin out.

There's music blarin upstairs. Some sort of miserable shit. But least she's in.

'Come in here and sit down, love,' Mum says. 'I'll make us a cuppa.'

I don't look round, and start straight up the stairs. 'John,' she says.

I stop.

'John, love.'

But I ain't turnin round.

Mum tells me Becky ain't had it easy since I been away, and that I might want to leave her for a bit. Have a cup of tea first, you know.

I know what she's sayin but I don't wanna hear this shit. Just wanna see my sister, so I carry on up.

Becky must've moved into my room cos that's where this fuckin miserable dirge is comin from. I knock on the door. But she ain't gonna hear with all that fuckin racket, so I turn the handle slow and go in.

Wall to wall posters. Siouxsie and the Banshees, The Cure, Sisters of Mercy. All that fuckin Goth shit. Becky's sittin on her bed, lookin at a magazine. Don't barely fuckin recognise her. Hair all dyed black and fuckin everywhere, face done up white as her fuckin bed sheets and this black make-up round her mouth and eyes. Dunno if she's heard me come in, but she ain't lookin up. I close the door soft and knock on the inside.

'Becks?' I says. 'It's me.'

She looks up like she don't care a fuck and goes back to her magazine.

'Becks, I'm home. Got out today.'

She shuts the magazine quick and chucks it on the floor. Storms over, givin me this filthy fuckin look like what I ain't never seen on her before. And then BANG. Smacks me round the fuckin face. Knocks me back a couple of steps. And me mouth's bleedin.

'What the fuck was that for?' I says.

She hits me again. Then blows up proper and starts screamin at me.

'What the fuck was that for? What the fuck was that for?'

The tears are streamin black down her face, and I know she's got the last seven years in each and every one of em.

I go to put me arm round her and she tells me not to fuckin touch her.

Fuck.

And just when I think I'm in for another slatin, her voice turns soft, soft like the child she still is.

'I needed you, Johnny,' she says. 'I fucking needed you.

And...and when Dad...'

I hang me head. I hang me head cos there ain't nothing else I can do.

And we stand there for what seems fuckin ages, but what probably ain't even a minute. And it's like, as I'm standin there, head bowed, I'm realisin what I done. What I really done, to me family. And I wanna take it all back. I wanna say it weren't my fault, and that it weren't really me what done them things, and that I was a messed up, fucked-up kid, cos all I wanted was my dad.

I wanna say all these things to Becky so it'll make it all better for her. But there's a lump in me throat and it's stoppin me from sayin any fuckin thing at all. I reach out for her, and I'm holdin her in me arms, and we're both sobbin like newborn fuckin babies.

I start thinkin of Mum downstairs, on her own. Her two kids. All she's got. Upstairs. Bound to be thinkin what we're talkin of. Bound to be thinkin we're talkin about her and Charlie. Even if we ain't. I tense up again, just thinkin of it.

'Becky?' I says, calm as I can, but I know me voice is in shreds. And I ask her about Mum and Charlie.

Nothing, for a bit. Then she pushes me away like she can't bear to have me near her and I'm back on me heels.

And she's at it again. Fuckin screamin her head off, tellin me I ain't got a fuckin clue what it's been like for her and Mum, me bein inside, and Dad not around. Reckons it's nearly killed Mum.

'And when I needed you,' she says, 'where were you? Got yourself banged up because all you could think about was your fucking self.'

Black tears startin up again. She's well out of control now, shakin so much she can't move.

She's run out of words and just stands there lookin right into me eyes, knowin there ain't no words she's ever gonna find that'll make her feel any better. I can't do nothing but stand there and take it. Take it all. And I tell you what, I tell you fuckin what, George Johnson and cunts like that, Ronnie Swordfish, they ain't got nothing on my sis. It's like she's openin me eyes and rubbin sand in em, and all I wanna do is rub em till they bleed.

***

Later, I'm downstairs with Mum, havin a cuppa. New china cups. Proper cups. Saucers and everything. And I know what Becky's sayin, about Mum and Charlie. But it don't make it none the fuckin easier.

Mum asks me if Becky's okay, and I tell her she is. But she knows she ain't. Must've heard every fuckin word upstairs.

After our second cuppa, after I've answered all her questions about how I am, and what I'm gonna do, and shit like that, me makin all of it up on the spot cos I ain't got a fuckin clue about none of it, we ain't got nothing more to say to each other. But I can't fuckin ignore it. Can't let it go. But I gotta go in sideways cos facin it head on's just too fuckin much.

I know he's shelled out for the carpets, that's pretty fuckin obvious, and probably the cups and loads more I don't fuckin know about, but I need her to tell me. I need her to fuckin say it.

'Doin well at the shop, Mum?' I says to her.

Tells me she's still on the tills, does a bit of overtime where she can, but there ain't much goin at the moment. Has another sip of tea.

I look at her how she used to look at me when I told her what I done at school, even though she knew I never went.

I ask her about the carpets, how she got hold of em.

She sips the last of her tea, and puts the cup and saucer on the table. Big smile, but sort of embarrassed.

Here it comes. Every breath fuckin hurts now. Like it did when that cunt of a judge sent us down all them years back and when Dad was lookin at me when I knew he was gone.

She's gonna say it. Charlie fuckin Paynter and my mum.

'That's not me, dear,' she says. 'That's Kenny.'

Fuckin what?

'Kenny?'

She tells me he moved in not long after his old girl got dragged dead out the River, and he's been sort of helpin out.

I wanna ask her all about him, how he is, what he's up to, and how the fuck he's in any position to be fuckin 'helpin out'. I gotta clear this money thing first cos it don't sound fuckin right to me. No way I'm havin my mum gettin mixed up in no dodgy shit.

'What d'you mean, "helpin out"?'

She puts her head down a bit, like whatever she's gotta say, she don't wanna look at me when she's sayin it.

'Me and your dad, John,' she says, 'after he lost his job, it was so hard.'

And she tells me how they barely got by, how she just made a little go a long way, an that. And how Dad cried every night, the state they were in.

Hearin Mum talkin about Dad like she's doin makes me know

she's always gonna love him, no matter who else comes on the scene. I turn me eyes to the floor, and I realise I'm sittin in his chair, holdin onto the arms, scratchin and scrapin em at the ends just like he used to.

'Making ends meet,' she says, 'just got impossible in the end, and we started getting behind with the rent, and . . . other things.'

Puts me back to the Cup Final tickets and Dad's drinkin, and how she's probably thinkin all these years if she hadn't of bought them tickets he'd still be with us now.

She said Dad knew of this bloke they could go to. Said the Council were gonna turn em out the house. Reckons her and Dad had no choice.

This geezer what she's talkin about, the one Dad said could help em out, he don't sound like no fuckin bank manager to me, and I've half a fuckin idea who she's on about.

'And the money you borrowed, Kenny's payin it off?'

'That's right, John.'

Her head's up, smilin again.

'He's a good boy, John,' she says. Tells me his mum would've been so proud.

Bollocks. I ain't buyin this shit.

I mean, Kenny?

I ask her where Kenny's gettin the money from, and if he's still Kenny, you know, mad as fuck.

Mum says Kenny's just 'different', that's all. Reckons his mum must've left something when she passed and that he wants to help out cos of that time we had him live with us when his old girl was in hospital.

Only thing Kenny got left from his old girl was a manky old cat and some piss smellin carpets. Unless she had a secret stash, which I fuckin doubt.

I ask her how much Kenny's givin her.

Tells me more than they need. Says Kenny's got the kindest heart in the world.

Wellin up now, she is. Says Kenny's different than what he used to be, not much of him left. Reckons the hospital's done him a right bad turn.

'He doesn't understand like you and me,' she says.

Never was a fuckin mastermind to fuckin start with, but she don't see that. Thinks he was born fuckin normal and it was the hospital what fucked him up. Started way before that, but I don't wanna get into that with her. Just wanna find out about the dough.

She said she had a really hard time tryin to get him to take back what she didn't need. Said he took it back in the end when Mum said his old girl would've liked him to have some for himself. He was nearly crying when she give it back, she reckons. Mum's lookin at the clock as she's talkin, like she's waitin for something.

Door bell goes.

And she's up, sort of flustered, and goes in the kitchen. Comes back with a bulgin envelope in her hand and goes to the front door. Couple minutes later she's back. Still flustered but tryin to cover it up. I go to the window, see who it was, and see Terry Wilkins strollin past. That sorts out for definite where her and Dad was gettin the money from.

I chase out the door, but can't see the fucker nowhere. Then I look across the street at Kenny's.

And I'm thinkin what it must've been like for Dad and Mum to be in hock to Ronnie Swordfish all them years, what it must have done to them. And that little girl, that little girl, she was only five fuckin years old.

I feel me eyes begin to widen and harden and that cold air comes blowin right through em again.

Time to sort this out.

CHAPTER TWENTY-TWO

One of the new Indian families is comin out next door. Fuckin hundreds of em, all standin on the path, and there's more on the way. Dunno if Mum's told em about me, or they just see it in me eyes, but they're lookin at me like I'm some fuckin serial killer or something. Still, what do I fuckin care? I walk straight past em and carry on across the road to Kenny's gaff. Wanna double check, you know. Make sure. But a quick butchers in the front window and it's fuckin clear there ain't no one about.

So, I'm headin for the boozer. See what I can find out there. Mind you, what with Kenny back, Charlie movin in on me mum, and her gettin mixed up with Ronnie fuckin Swordfish, gettin hammered's the only thing makes fuckin sense about now. But as I'm gettin closer, I'm thinkin if it's such a good idea. I mean, I was sent down for havin a knife to some old girl's throat who was old enough to be me mum, and that sort of thing don't go down well round here. Goin for a copper, I think they'd swallow that, but not an old girl. But, fuck it. I done me time. Ain't I? I ain't expectin no fuckin welcome home party or nothing, banners and shit, you know. All I want's a fuckin pint.

I blow out me cheeks and go in. Least it's gonna be warmer in here.

Tony's servin a punter. He looks over at me soon as I come in, like he's expectin me. But he don't do nothing, just carries on pourin some geezer his pint. Don't take his eyes off me, though. Dribblin Albert proppin up the bar at the far end, wearin a dodgy-lookin syrup. Dad's factory mates, they're dotted about, and some of em off the market. Apart from Albert's new syrup, it's like fuckin walkin back in time.

As I'm headin for the bar, there's a hand comes on me shoulder from behind.

'Son?'

It's me Uncle Derek. I turn round, and he looks fuckin awful. Hair's all thinned out, and he's got these black bulges under his eyes like he ain't slept for fuckin years, and he looks so fuckin scrawny.

'Your Auntie Ivy and your Auntie Gwen's sittin over there,' he says.

He nods his head to a table in the corner by the door.

'Your mum said you probably be poppin in.'

I'm smilin over at me aunties, and they're both wavin back, grinnin at me like a pair of fuckin idiots. Don't know if they're pleased to see me or fuckin terrified. They're both wavin that stupid sort of wave all mums and aunties do when you're a kid, really quick and frantic, like the Queen Mum on speed.

'What you want, son?' Uncle Derek says, holdin up a fiver.

'Pint of bitter, please, Uncle Derek. Cheers.'

He tells me to sit down with me aunties, that he won't be a minute.

Me Auntie Ivy gets up and Auntie Gwen shoves over a bit when I come over, and I drop down between em.

Auntie Ivy leans in, gives me a peck on the cheek. She tries to put her arms round me, but sort of stops herself, and sits back.

'You're looking well, love,' she says.

But it don't feel like she's even talkin to me. It's like she's just sayin the words, and they sort of crumble in the air soon as they come out her mouth.

'Isn't he, Ivy?' Auntie Gwen says, sort of too fuckin full on to be fuckin believable. 'I mean, you know, all things considering.'

And there it is. There it fuckin is. All things considerin. He's just come out the nick after seven fuckin years for havin a knife to an old girl's throat then goin for a load of coppers, so all things considerin, the fact he ain't fuckin glassed the fuckin pair of us by now, well, that's a fuckin touch, ain't it? All things con-fuckin-siderin.

And all these cunts here. Not one of em's worth pissin on.

Auntie Ivy's lookin over at the bar where Uncle Derek's still waitin, and Auntie Gwen's fiddlin about in her handbag.

Pub door opens. In walks Kenny. Looks like shit. Hair all shaved off. Baggy tracksuit bottoms, shitty green anorak torn all to fuck at the arms. And he's fuckin huge. Huger than when I saw him last. He's like a fuckin elephant. And all these people, all these people he's walkin through, they're smilin at him, big and wide, and they're sayin, 'All right, Kenny?', and 'How you doin, Kenny?', and they're slappin him on the back, and they fuckin love him.

'Oh, he's such a nice boy, that young Kenny,' Auntie Gwen says. 'Isn't he Ive?'

Auntie Ivy's lookin at Kenny as if he's some sort of fuckin film star or something, you know, eyes all gone big and fuckin glazed over and shit.

'And after all he's been through,' Auntie Gwen says.

It's like they forgot I'm even fuckin here.

Kenny's standin at the bar now, and Uncle Derek's talkin to him. Kenny looks over at me. Nothing on his face. Fuckin nothing. Fucker ain't right. Clocked that a long time back. Tony lands a coke on the bar in front of him, and Kenny downs it in one and goes straight back out the boozer like he's in some sort of fuckin hurry. Don't even pay for his drink.

I gotta go after him, see what the fucker's up to. I sit tight a couple of seconds so it ain't too fuckin obvious I'm on his case.

Uncle Derek's back with the drinks.

'Sorry, Uncle Derek,' I says, squeezin out from me Aunties. 'Promised Mum I'd only be a while, you know? See you later.'

Soon as I say it, I see they're fuckin thinkin I'm some sort of rude cunt who ain't changed his fuckin ways for no one. And, you know, maybe I fuckin ain't.

Outside, Kenny's nowhere in sight. It's fuckin pissin down and, fuckin bollocks, I've left me coat inside. But I ain't goin back in there. No fuckin way. And no way I'm goin home cos I'll just have me mum fussin round me, makin me cups of bleedin tea all night and drivin me fuckin mad. Besides, Charlie's probably round by now, seein how it all went.

And I gotta keep movin cos the standin still's fuckin killin me.

So, I'm walkin. Walkin in the rain and the wind and the cold. Anywhere. And me Doc Martens are smackin on the pavement, echoin like an empty heartbeat. And I tell you what, that's the loneliest sound in the whole fuckin world.

I'm closin me eyes as I walk now, and I'm in the dark, just me and that sound, and I'd do anything to break it in two. Anything. I open me eyes and start runnin.

For a while the sound gets louder, the smackin becomes a poundin and the poundin a crashin. And the rain's cuttin in me face like nails from a cannon, and I'm fightin against the wind, and I'm fightin against meself. It's like everything's rushin past me all at once; shops, lamp-posts, houses, parked cars, and I wanna know what it's like to never stop runnin, to hear me lungs burst, to feel me face smashin into the pavement.

There's just pain now. Chest, side, head. Just pain. And through it all, I keep on runnin, skiddin round corners, crossin empty streets, and I can't hear nothing no more. And every couple of seconds I close me eyes just so I can feel.

I'm turnin into the Bethnal Green Road. Cars everywhere, headlights blurred in the rain. And some fucker's crawlin across the road on his hands and knees through a fuckin river. Must be pissed or stoned or mental or something. Car horns blarin, people windin down their windows, all shoutin at him. I'm slowin down a bit cos he's lookin at me. And I sort of recognise him. He ain't sayin nothing, just lookin. And then I see it's Jimmy fuckin Lawson, from school, the geezer what done up the Baby Jesus' face with Smarties and a fag.

I'm stoppin, slowin down. He's callin me over, wavin me to him. But I can't hear nothing but the sound of me own wheezin. And I'm lookin at Jimmy Lawson and I ain't never see such a state in all me fuckin life. If it weren't for the fact he's out here on his hands and knees, I'd swear by the look on his face he was fuckin drownin.

And I keep on runnin.

The rain's lettin up, but I'm soaked to the skin, and I'm shiverin. Can't run no more. I'm dead on me feet. Stumblin. Ain't even walkin straight, and me bones is shiverin and achin, and I dunno where the fuck I'm goin.

I stagger on through the dark, blind and in tears.

***

Dunno how I got here, but I'm standin outside the gates of the London City Crematorium, where they put Dad. The iron gates are shut. A big fuck-off padlock makin sure it stays that way. I fall to me knees and I'm lookin through the bars, holdin on tight, and it scares the shit outta me cos I dunno if I'm on the outside lookin in or on the inside lookin out. I'm like that fuckin ages, and at the end all I wanna do is see me mum. Hold her close.

I go home past The Barmy, jump the fence, and go and sit on the swings for a while. Don't seem like yesterday since we was all playin football up there on the slope with Dad and all me mates. And that time when Kenny goes in goal and makes a tit of himself and Robbie Jenkins scrapes his leg cross the tree in a tackle and has to go home with his jumper tied round his knee to stop the blood pissin out. Don't seem like fuckin yesterday.

And no one ever tells you stuff like that's gonna end. Not your mum, not your dad, not your teachers. Fuckin no one. I mean, you know nothin lasts forever, you know that, but that's sort of different, that's sort of in your head. But you don't know it inside, you know, deep down. And when it happens, when it all goes to fuck, that's when you know you don't get none of it back. That's when you know you're on your fuckin own.

**

It's early hours when I'm comin down our street. Passed Thommo's gaff on the way. Front garden's all grown over and the windows are boarded up and the front door's got graffiti all over it. Old man's done a runner or banged up, that's fuckin obvious. And poor old Thommo, cos he got sectioned, he ain't even got a fuckin lettin out date. Just another poor cunt, like the rest of us.

Cos there's holes in this world, see. Holes. And the likes of Thommo, and Keith, and me, and Kenny, we just sort of fall through em. We weren't never bad kids, we just didn't have nothing to hold on to, that's all.

I'm outside Kenny's, about to cross over, when the street lamp buzzes and goes out, then it comes on again, sort of like it's talkin to me. I stop and look at it, at the light. And I'm tryin to see what Kenny see all them years back, that Christmas when it was pissin down with rain and I got me Raleigh Chopper.

I know he see something cos it was writ all over his face. Me, I can't see fuck all.

I cross over home, and let meself in.

The little light's on in the front room and the curtains are open a bit. Mum's asleep in Dad's chair and the telly's gone all white noise where she's fell asleep waitin up for me. I go over and pull the curtains to, quiet, so I don't wake her up. And without thinkin, I find meself lookin over at Kenny's.

And there's his face. At the bedroom window. Starin into the street lamp.

Mum's woke up behind me, and yawns.

'You all right, love?' she says. Then she sees the state I'm in. Tells me I'll catch me death and goes to fetch a towel.

I don't turn round. Can't get me eyes off Kenny. I wanna go over there. Have it out with him. But I've got this cold sweat come over me, and I'm shiverin like fuck with the cold and the rain.

'He's up there all the time,' Mum says, back with a towel, dryin me hair from behind, slowly, her fingers pressing in. I shut me eyes. 'Funny,' she says, 'it's like he's looking for something the way he stares out of that window, don't you think? It's just the saddest thing.'

I'm thinkin, it's sad and it ain't. I mean, it's sad when you look at it from the outside, but when you really look at Kenny, you know, really look, it's the only time he ever fuckin comes alive.

'Do you remember when he was here?' Mum says, half a laugh comin out the same time as a yawn. 'I used to catch him in our room all the time, looking across at that light. Used to drive your father mad.'

I nod me head, smilin at the thought of me dad gettin pissed off with Kenny bein in their bedroom, and I drop the curtain and turn round.

And there's Mum, lookin at me same way Kenny's lookin at that street lamp. It's like I'm fillin her up, sort of shinin in her eyes.

'Have my bed tonight, dear,' she says. 'You need a proper night's sleep. Look at you."

Yeah, I'm thinkin. Look at me.

I see there's some blankets and a pillow piled up one end of the settee she's put for herself. But turfin me own mum out her bed me first night back, bless her, after all I done to her? I won't have none of that, and she's too tired to argue.

She yawns again, covers her mouth as she's doin it, and heads off to bed.

'Goodnight, dear,' she says, from the doorway.

I nod me head again, this time with a lump in me throat. And when she's gone, I peel off me clothes, climb onto the settee and wrap myself up so tight I can't fuckin move.

CHAPTER TWENTY-THREE

Next day, I'm shiverin and achin and coughin up phlegm. In bed a week. Mum's bed. She's kippin on the settee. I feel bad for it, I really fuckin do, but she won't have it no other way. Not that I'm up to arguin or nothing. Makes me a flask of minestrone before she goes to work, and Becky's up and down stairs all day with hot drinks and fillin up me water bottle. I'm knocked out first couple of days, overdosed on Lemsip and headache tablets, but after that I'm on the mend pretty quick.

Even gettin used to that miserable fuckin Goth shit Becky spends half her life listenin to. It's so fuckin bleak, after a while, gets sort of comfortin, you know. Has her door open all day for the phone and the front door, so I get it pretty much constant.

***

Towards the end of the week, Auntie Gwen and Uncle Derek and Auntie Ivy come round for a cuppa. I'm feelin better and Charlie's here, keepin a low profile, joinin in here and there, but mostly just smilin and noddin and stuff. We're talkin about old times and about Dad and Grandad and Nan and we're laughin and next minute we're quiet and sad, and then we're laughin again. Charlie knowed em all, through the boozer an that. And he was good mates with Dad for years.

Becky's upstairs playin her music and we're all sayin it's not real music, not proper music, not like Elvis, you know, proper music, and Mum says what a good kid she is and Auntie Ivy and Auntie Gwen says Dad would've been so proud how she's come out like she has. So fuckin proud. And then it goes sort of quiet, and I know they're all thinkin, all wonderin, what the fuck Dad would've made of me.

Mum sees it in me face, and says for me and Charlie to go and make another pot. Give us a both a break. She gives me her cup, and Charlie gets the others.

***

I've opened the back door and I'm havin a fag. Charlie's fillin up the kettle. As it's boilin, he's tellin me he's got hold of a pitch at Romford. Wants to know if I wanna help him out Wednesdays, Fridays and Saturdays and do Brick Lane on me own of a Sunday. He's offerin a ton a week for the privilege.

I'm listenin, and I ain't. Cos there's something I need to say to him. Words in the dark, cuttin themselves loose.

'So what you say, John?' he says. 'You up for it?'

Love Mum to bits, I do, but I don't wanna be stuck round here all me fuckin life, and without a bit of tank, that's where I'm fuckin endin up. I tell him I'll do it. He looks so fuckin relieved, like his fuckin life's on it, so I know Mum's put him up to it.

But I'm breakin inside. And them words I gotta say, it's like they're made of razor blades and the harder I'm pushin em down the deeper they're cuttin me to fuckin shreds. Cos I know once I say em, it all ends.

'Charlie?' I says.

He's lookin at me like a little boy. I swear, this big fuckin lump of a geezer's tremblin in his boots. And cos he's tremblin I know he loves her more than anything in the whole fuckin world.

'Look after Mum,' I says.

He breathes deep and walks over, puts his massive arm round me shoulders.

And the weight of that arm opens me right up inside.

***

Couple of weeks go by, and everything's tickin over sweet as a fuckin nut. Romford's took off like a dream, and I'm rushed off me feet at Brick Lane.

Keeps me off the streets, as me nan used to say. God bless her.

Charlie's here at the market first Sunday, but he don't work the stall. Leaves me to that. Helps set up then goes round the other stalls talkin all day long.

And I'm in the boozer most nights. Good as gold they are with me now. Good as fuckin gold. Just wanted to make a point when I come out, that's all. Wanted to let me know what I done weren't fuckin big and it weren't fuckin clever, and if I thought I was gonna come strollin back out of nick after all them years like nothing fuckin happened, I got another fuckin think comin. So when I slinks out the boozer that first night, with me tail between me legs, that's all they wanted to see. Like I says, good as gold after that. Every fuckin one of em.

It's me second Sunday at Brick Lane and I'm doin a blindin trade. Becky's buyin a couple of tapes from Eddie Cox opposite. She's always hangin round the market with her mates, buyin all sorts of bits of crap. Right Gothed up she is, now she's left school. Got her nose pierced, and her mouth, this big fuck-off cross hangin round her neck, full-on fuckin face paint, wearin nothing but black.

Eddie says to me he ain't see nothing like it, other than them Hammer Horror films we watched as kids. Shakes his head, he does. Old fashioned, is Eddie, even though he's only a couple years older than me. Says he dunno what the world's comin to. Mind you, he can talk. Spends half his life chained to a fuckin dungeon up in Soho gettin the fuckin shit beat out of him by some granny in high heels. Still, takes all sorts.

Fuckin weirdo.

Becky's come over. She's left her mates at the stall, and Eddie's givin em all the spiel, and they're lookin at him like he's some sort of fuckin idiot.

'All right, Becks?' I says. 'What you got there?'

She hands over one of the tapes. Unknown Pleasures. Joy Division. Now that's a fuckin lot who wouldn't know an unknown pleasure if it hit him em in the fuckin face. I give it back to her and she sticks it in her pocket.

'What's the other one?'

She tells me it's Shakin Stevens.

I piss meself.

'Shakin Stevens?'

'It's for Mum,' she says. 'She likes him.'

And I never even knew my mum liked Shakin Stevens, and I feel like shit. Becks looks round to see if her mates is comin but they've gone off without her.

'Best be goin,' she says.

I tell her I'll see her later, and that I'm really sorry about the Shakin Stevens thing.

She smiles, sort of seein the funny side, her dressed up like the Bride of fuckin Frankenstein with a Shakin Stevens tape in her pocket.

I ain't felt this good in ages. Feels like I'm on a clean slate, you know, got a chance to start over. Ain't seen Kenny since he run out the pub that time. Worried about him first off, you know, when I found out he was out the nut-house, but I got me own life to live. Can't worry about him no more. He's a big boy now. A big fuckin boy. And I mean, who cares where he's gettin his money from and what he does with it, and where he fuckin goes at night? So fuckin what. He's doin okay. And Mum. She's got Charlie, and Becky's a good kid and I'm settin myself straight again. Even Mum owin Ronnie Swordfish ain't a problem cos Kenny's coverin that, so everything's fuckin cushty.

And the girl who was five years old, I ain't thought of her in fuckin ages.

I'm even gettin back into the football again. I was inside when we come third in the First Division. The whole fuckin league – higher than Arsenal was when they played us at Wembley. And missin that season, suddenly, it fuckin hurts. It's sort of hit me there's years of me life – whole football seasons – I ain't never gettin back again.

I'm getting to midweek games where I can. Can't get to Saturdays cos of the market, but I follow the Hammers through the papers and on the telly and with all me heart. Would love to get down regular, but Dad did that shit job in the factory for years cos he had to. Least I can do is stick it out at the market. Cuts me in two standin here when there's a match on, but fills me heart up an all, you know, thinkin how proud Dad'd be, me doin it the hard way to bring some money in for Mum.

Becky's sayin something to me, but I ain't listenin. I'm lookin right past her cos there's this face movin through the crowd, comin straight at me. I go cold all over. He's gettin closer, and he's got that same slimy fuckin grin he's always had. There's me thinkin about Mum owin Ronnie Swordfish, when I remember it's me owes him more than any fuckin one I know.

Here he is. Terry Wilkins.

'Johnny fuckin Sissons.'

'All right, Terry,' I says.

Was only a matter of time.

He asks me how I am, said he tried poppin round a while back, but Becky told him to fuck off.

Becky gives him a proper filthy look, which ain't hard in her get-up. Makes him fuckin edgy, I can see that. These two have definitely had previous. And she just keeps on starin, Becky. Just like what Kenny used to.

'Ain't you gotta run along, little girl?' Terry says, right nasty.

Becky don't say a word.

I ask Terry what he wants. Like I don't fuckin know. He turns his back on Becky and smiles big and slimy.

'Fuck me, John,' he says, 'thought you'd be pleased to see me, you know?'

It's all comin back. Five years old. Five fuckin years old.

'Tell him to fuck off, John,' Becky says, not takin her eyes off him.

Terry carries on like she ain't even there.

'Thought we might have a chat, mate, you know, about old times.'

Old times. I bet he fuckin does.

I wanna tell him to fuck off, like Becky's sayin, but I know he ain't come on his own back. And I don't want my little sister gettin any fuckin wind of what Ronnie Swordfish done for me.

'It's all right, Becks,' I says to her, all big brotherly, 'I'll see you later. Tell Mum I'll be in about six.'

She looks at me cold for a couple of seconds then turns round and walks off slow.

I ask Terry again what he wants. He says he's told Ronnie Swordfish all about me, and he wants to see me pronto.

Lizzie's come over from next door, and she's givin Wilkins the same look what Becky give him. I know his little brother always was a nasty little shit, but seems Terry here's in a whole different fuckin league.

I tell Terry he'll have to give me a minute while I sort things out, and I ask Lizzy to mind the stall for me.

'It's all right, mate,' he says. 'Got all the time in the world.'

I sort things out with Lizzie. Don't take long, but I'm stretchin it out like I just wanna hold onto this last little bit. The bit when everything seemed so fuckin handsome.

***

And we're walkin fast and all the time, Terry don't stop fuckin talkin.

Tells me how the Firm's in a bit of lumber, how they've lost some good lads inside, and in other ways. Names I never fuckin heard of. Tidy O'Leary, Vinnie Baker, Pete the Hatchet. Says they're all doin some fuckin hefty bird. Then he says about some geezer name Chunky Warren. Said Ronnie had no fuckin choice with Chunky. Broke his bleedin heart to do it, it did. Yeah, I bet it fuckin did.

We come off Brick Lane at Old Montague Street, then down Greatorex Street and across the Whitechapel Road.

Terry carries on talkin bollocks, like he's Al Pacino.

'And it's like the whole game ain't holdin up so well, now, you know, John,' he says, 'right across the fuckin board. I mean there's fuckers lookin to move in all over the shop. There's some lessons need teachin, Johnny son, and we're fuckin thin on the ground.' Wanker. 'So when I tells Ronnie about you, how you was standin up to them screws in nick, how they just couldn't fuckin break you, and how I knew you from school and what a handful you was there, he says to me, "Terrence", he says to me, "Terrence, my son, now there's a boy I like the fuckin sound of".'

Plumbers Row. Coke Street. Weyhill Road. All of it a shit-hole.

'And once you're in with Ronnie, John,' he says, 'you ain't gonna want for fuckin nothing. He's a good bloke. Old school. Believes in payin a fair fuckin wage for a fair fuckin day's work. Even the patsies down the track are on half a monkey a week, and that's just for puttin on a couple of fuckin wagers.'

Half a monkey a week? Fuck me. And then I'm thinkin, you know, I do owe the geezer for that cunt Johnson, and the least I can do is hear him out. And I know she was only five years old, bless her, but there ain't nothing I can do about that now.

'What's Harry up to these days, Terry?' I says to him as we're dodgin motors on the Commercial Road. And just sayin that little arsehole's name makes me wanna find him and punch his fuckin lights out, rememberin what he did to Kenny.

Terry stops.

'We don't talk about him,' he says, dead fuckin serious.

'No?'

'No.'

Well, I've touched a fuckin nerve there, cos from then on, the cunt don't say a fuckin word. We sprint across Cable Street. Back Church Lane. Long old stretch.

We're comin into the wastelands of Wapping. Where the Tobacco Dock used to be. Just one big fuckin buildin site now. And we're treadin over rubble and girders and all sorts of shit. There's a couple of diggers about, but there ain't no one in em. There ain't no one nowhere. Just one big fuckin wasteland of shit.

And there's this Portacabin right in the middle of it.

'So why's he called Ronnie Swordfish?' I says, as we're clamberin over this mound of fuckin dirt. 'I mean, it ain't his real name or nothing, is it?'

Terry says, 'Course it fuckin ain't.'

He's proper turned since I said about his little cunt of a brother.

Then he tells me Ronnie Swordfish is called Ronnie Swordfish because he's a Pisces.

There's me thinkin this Ronnie Swordfish geezer's gonna be some bleedin fuckin psycho or something. And I smile to meself, sort of relieved.

'His name is Ronnie,' Terry says, sort of exasperated, 'he carries a sword and he's a Pisces. Ronnie. Sword. Fish. Get it?'

A sword?

Fuck.

CHAPTER TWENTY-FOUR

As we're gettin nearer the Portacabin, I see a big fuck-off knuckle-dragger standin guard outside.

'All right, Brooksy?' Terry says, tryin to talk hard, but I can tell he's fuckin terrified of this cunt. 'Tell the Governor I got Johnny Sissons with me.'

Brooksy gives Terry a look like he fuckin hates him. Sort of leerin, like he wants to rip his arms off here and now, throw him in the fuckin River, and wave to him as he drowns. But he don't. Not this time. Instead, he knocks on the Portacabin door. The door opens a crack, and Brooksy says a few words I can't hear.

Then out comes this bloke. Normal lookin. Mid-sixties. Suited up, but not like them Mafia types off the films, just a normal brown suit. He comes over to me and Terry, all friendly, arms out, like he's known me all his fuckin life.

'Johnny,' he says, ignorin Terry and clappin me on the top of me arms with his hands. His hands are massive. And he's got a smile like me Grandad, sort of like his eyes are smilin as much as his mouth. 'It's a pleasure to meet you, son.'

He puts his arm around me shoulders and leads me towards the Portacabin. Brooksy opens the door, and we go inside.

***

The Portacabin's just like a little office. Ronnie sits down behind a desk at one end. There's a couple of other blokes sittin at a table up the other end, smokin cigars and lookin proper fuckin scary. Terry sits down with em, but you can see he ain't comfortable. He's way out his depth with these bastards, and he knows they'd cut his throat soon as look at him.

'Get the boy a drink, George,' Ronnie says. Asks me if Scotch is all right.

I says it is.

He tells me to sit down and make meself at home.

George brings me drink over and lands it on the desk in front of me.

'Right,' Ronnie says, givin me that big friendly smile of his. 'I'll cut to the chase, son. Terrence here has told me all about you, and although the other lads reckon he is a Grade 'A' Mister fucking Wanker – and who knows, they might have a point – I like him. He's a good boy.'

As he's talkin to me, I can't help thinkin of me Grandad.

'The minute I saw you, John,' he says, 'I knew young Terrence hadn't let me down. It's in your eyes. I see that look in the best of em.'

Here he sort of stares off for a second, like he's rememberin or he's lost his track or something. Then he carries on like he ain't even realised he's done it.

'And I warrant you're no fucking idiot, neither, kid. Not like Brooksy out there. Has his uses, Brooksy, wouldn't be without the cunt, but he's somewhat limited, if you know what I mean. Good job and all, cos if he had half a brain, we'd all be propping up the bleeding flyover, wouldn't we lads?'

The other blokes laugh, sort of deep, like an animal would laugh. Terry joins in but he stands out a fuckin mile.

'Now, John,' Ronnie carries on, 'I don't know if young Terrence here has told you, but we've had a few problems of late.'

'He mentioned it,' I says.

Ronnie leans back in his chair and puts his hands behind his head.

'I've got a very delicate situation needs sorting, John,' he says. 'Pains me to say it, John, fucking kills me, but I think we've got someone on the Firm doing the dirty on old Ronnie.'

I find that fuckin hard to believe. I mean, on the one hand, he seems a pretty reasonable sort of bloke and if everyone's gettin weighed out like Terry reckons, why the fuck would anyone wanna be skimmin off the top? And on the other hand, he's obviously a fuckin maniac. With a sword. Fuck me, whatever silly cunt's rippin him off really has gotta be some sort of fuckin idiot.

He says if I help him out there'll be no lookin back for me. And I reckon if I don't, lookin won't even be a fuckin option.

He leans forward towards me, like he's gonna tell me a secret.

'Son,' he says, lookin genuinely fuckin aggrieved. 'We've got a problem with Kenny.'

Shit.

'Kenny?'

Ronnie blows his cheeks out and shakes his head, and sits back again.

'Couldn't believe it myself, son, when I heard,' he says, and carries on his little performance. 'Breaks my bleeding heart. Don't know how he's doing it. Can't work it out for the life of me. I mean, he's thicker than Brooksy out there, and that takes some fucking doing, I can tell you, but I just can't work it out. Mind you, they say some of these mong sorts have got fucking genius in em, don't they, John?'

Sort of makes sense now, where Kenny's been gettin all that money from.

Ronnie says how he's got 'a little interest' in the dogs, a 'business venture'. Walthamstow, Romford, Catford, all over the city. He's got patsies on each track layin down the cash and the likes of Kenny goes along at the end of the night and brings back his winnins.

'I mean,' Ronnie says, 'you and me, John, we both know Kenny's soft as shit, don't we? But he's a big old bastard and those eyes of his, they fucking scare the shit out of me sometimes, so I know none of the patsies are gonna fuck with him. You know what I mean?'

I hear chairs movin behind me, footsteps, and the door opens and shuts. Ronnie don't take his eyes off me, so I don't dare fuckin turn round.

'A little dickie bird tells me,' Ronnie says, 'young Kenny's been flashing his cash, you know, handing it out to all and fucking sundry.'

He tells me that's nice of him. Really fuckin nice. But it's hurtin him. Says it's bad for business. Reckons there's only one place Kenny can be gettin the money from. And that's old Ronnie himself.

If Kenny's helpin other people out, you know, not just Mum, people who might otherwise be regular customers of Mr Ronald Swordfish here, I can see how it might be gettin up his arse.

'And what do you want me to do?' I says.

Ronnie puts on his proper sorry look.

'I know Kenny's a mate of yours,' he says, 'and, believe me, he's like a fucking son to me, like me own fucking boy. You know what I mean?'

He blows out his cheeks and shakes his head, like he genuinely can't fuckin believe someone's been nickin off him.

'I need you to bring him in, John, so we can have a chat. Just a chat. Will you do that for me, John?'

He could have Kenny down here in a fuckin heartbeat, I know that. He knows that. But he wants to know if I'm on the fuckin level. He's fuckin testin me. The bastard wants to know if I got what it takes. Wants to know if I'll shop me nearest and dearest on his fuckin say so. But it'd be like walkin Kenny to the fuckin gallows and puttin the rope round his head me fuckin self. Ain't no way I'm doin that. No fuckin way.

'And if I don't?' I says.

He sits up again, straight. And smiles like me Grandad.

***

Don't take me long to get lost comin back. This side of the Commercial Road's off me manor, and I ain't got a clue where I'm goin. Besides, me head's spinnin and I can't think straight to save me fuckin life.

All I know is I gotta find Kenny. But when I gets down our street, his gaff's all dark like it always is.

Fuck. Fuck. Fuck.

I gotta think this one out.

I get home just as Mum's clearin up the tea stuff. Becky's at the sink in the kitchen givin me a filthy look.

'There's a plate of sandwiches in the fridge for you, love,' Mum says. 'And some crisps in the cupboard.'

I don't say nothing back. Ain't hungry no more. I go in the front room and sit myself in Dad's chair. Mum comes in, tea-towel in her hand ready to dry up.

She asks me if everything's all right, if there's anything I wanna talk about.

She's sayin it the way she used to when I was a kid, like she knows there's something up but wants me to tell her myself. I'm guessin Becky's told her I see Terry Wilkins.

I tell her I'm all right, just a bit tired.

She knows I'm lyin through me teeth.

She's says she's puttin the kettle on and to give her a shout if I want a cuppa.

I tell her thanks.

I need something a bleedin sight stronger than a fuckin cuppa to get through this.

Me brain's goin hundred miles a second, tryin to get a way out of the shit I'm in. The shit me and Kenny's both in. But the way I sees it, there's only one way this is endin.

I'm lookin out the window at Kenny's. And the light from the street lamp outside his house is on the flicker again.

Ronnie's leavin it twenty-four hours before he wants me to bring Kenny in. And I know it ain't cos of the kindness of his heart. He's givin me a chance to tip Kenny off. That's what it is. Like the bastard's wantin me to fuck up, so either way, he can have his fuckin bloodbath. Wants me down the boozer tomorrow night when Kenny comes in. Says there's gonna be a phone call, then wants me to follow Kenny down the wasteland. Make sure he gets there. That's all. Case there's any funny business, case I get any ideas, Ronnie says he'll have a couple of his lads down the boozer keepin an eye on proceedings.

Thinkin hard as I can, hard as I ever thought, but nothing's happenin.

But if I can find out where Kenny's stashin the dosh, have a strong old word with him, you know, put the frighteners on him, make sure he knocks his little scam on the head, then that's bound to fuckin sort it. Ronnie's happy cos he's back in pocket, I'm fuckin square with the psycho-fucker, Kenny gets a slap on the wrist, and it's happy families all round.

Fuckin sorted.

But I got this empty sort of feelin like I know I'm kiddin myself, but it's the best I can come up with under the circumstances. Becky comes in, givin me the same look she give Wilkins at the stall.

'Mum's asking if you want a cup of tea,' she says, cold as fuckin anything.

'Tell Mum not to wait up,' I says, and I'm out the house in seconds.

CHAPTER TWENTY-FIVE

The lights are still off when I get to Kenny's. Never would've reckoned on him havin the brains to turn someone like Ronnie Swordfish over. Still don't believe it, but then Kenny always was a closed fuckin book. It's them eyes of his. Like blacked-out car windows. Fuckin worryin when you think about it. It's like I don't even know him no more.

I ring the bell. No answer. I ain't got time to fuck about.

Quick look round. Empty street. Door frame's rotted to fuck, quick shove and the door pops open. I reckon puttin the lights on's the best start. If Kenny comes in I'll just blag it. Burglars, fire, gas, fuckin anything.

Place is even more of a shit-hole than what I remember. Kinda scary an all, to think this is where he actually lives. Probably better than livin on the streets and goin down the bins for your dinner, but only fuckin just.

Me feet's scrapin on the floor on account of the carpet bein pulled up. With the state I saw it last, I'm not fuckin surprised. Only the newspaper's left, you know, like they used to have under carpets, keep the place warm. And I'm glad to get off it in the front room. But the front room's bloody freezin. Just like it always was.

And there, sittin on this manky sleepin bag in the middle of the floor, starin blind at a wall, is Kenny.

Looks better than when I saw him last, I mean really saw him – the pub don't count. Last time I see him proper was down Petticoat Lane with his head in a bin, so anything's a fuckin improvement on that I suppose. He's lookin at me kinda funny, like he's tryin to remember something. His eyes are all watered over, but he's always had that. Funny, forgot how fuckin weird it looks, like he's always on the edge of either cryin or screamin.

The settee's gone, no telly, no nothing. Nothing other than this tatty old sleepin bag in the middle of the floor, empty crisp bags and other shit all round it.

I sit on the floor by the door, me knees up to me chin.

Kenny's fiddlin with his hands, lookin at em, like he don't know what to say.

'Kenny?' I says.

He's lookin up at me now, scared, like he's in for a right fuckin hidin.

I come right to the point. I know there ain't no money come from his old girl peggin it. Not lookin at the state of this place, and the state of Kenny. Knew that soon as Mum said. So what the fuck is he up to? Gettin in with Ronnie Swordfish for a start, I mean, for fuck's sake, that cunt blows people up in cars. And that ain't nothing I want me mum anything fuckin close to. Nor Kenny, come to that.

He's answered all me other questions, you know, how he's coped all these years, and stuff, just by lookin at him. He's fucked. Poor cunt's come out fuckin worse than I have, and that's fuckin sayin something the way I feel deep down. Seein him sittin here brings it all back.

'Kenny?'

He looks away again, back to his hands on his lap. He's smilin a little bit, just a touch, but he still ain't sayin a word.

Gotta tell him how it is. Lay it on the fuckin line.

'Kenny,' I says, gettin right fuckin uppity now, 'I ain't havin Mum involved in nothing fuckin bent, all right? So just tell me what the fuck's goin on. That's all I wanna know. And fuckin give Ronnie his money back. I'll sort out the rest.'

Smile's gone now. He's lookin right at me. Then slowly, and sort of stutterin, he tells me he's just helpin out. That's all. Just helpin out. Won't say nothing else.

I can see I'm bangin me head on a fuckin brick wall with this one. Like talkin to a fuckin imbecile. Makes me think of Thommo, like in court, and I'm wonderin what sort of a fuckin mess that poor cunt's in. And Keith. And I can't think of either one of em without fillin up.

I'm lookin dead in Kenny's eyes now, and it's sendin me a million fuckin miles away. And I'm with Thommo, and me mates, and we're seven years old, runnin round over The Barmy havin a kick-about with Dad, and now Keith's there, and we're sittin in the back of the class at Isaac Meade, pissin ourselves laughin at something one of us has just said. Then I see the two of em in me room after Dad died, and they're tryin so fuckin hard to make it right. I close me eyes to blink out the tears, and I can feel Kenny starin at me. When I open me eyes again, he's got a tear, just one single tear, I fuckin swear it, just gettin ready to run down the side of his face.

Closest I ever see him come.

'See you round, Kenny,' I says, and I get up to go.

But he don't say nothing. Just sits there starin straight past me.

***

I ain't goin without the money, though. Even if I gotta tip the whole fuckin place upside down.

There's nothing in the back room, and the kitchen's bare. I'm in the hallway now, just about to go upstairs, when . . . BANG BANG BANG.

Footsteps beltin down the street, gettin nearer.

I'm holdin me breath at the bottom of the stairs lookin out the glass in the front door. Waitin. Dunno why, but I'm sort of expectin a key in the door or something, see Kenny's mum come waltzin in. A shadow goes quick past the glass and the footsteps keep on goin. I leg it up the stairs two at a time.

It's dead up here. Cold. Kenny's old bedroom's most likely. So in I go.

Ain't got no need to turn the light on cos the street lamp's lightin everything up. There's a bed frame with no mattress, Kenny's old wardrobe, and fuck all else. Easy to see there ain't nothing under the bed cos you can see right through the top. I open the wardrobe. And at the bottom, under a load of old hangers there's a sports bag. Same as I had when I was a kid with me football kit.

But this one's fuckin bulgin.

The street lamp flickers and goes out. Fuck. Room's so black I can't see me hand in front of me face. Comes on again a second later, but I'm shittin myself. Really fuckin shittin myself.

I grab hold of the bag. It's heavier than what I thought. I'm on the floor now, me back to the wall under the window. I open the zip.

It's stuffed full with loads and loads of books. Exercise books. You know, the ones you get at school. The sort Kenny had as a kid. And each one of these books has got 'My Diary' writ on it, and a date underneath. I take em out and stack em up round me. There's fuckin loads of em. Quick flick through shows they go back about fifteen years, right from when I first saw Kenny come tumblin out his house when we was nippers.

I know this ain't what I'm lookin for, it ain't the cash, but I got the feelin in these books, writ on these pages, is everything I need to get me and Kenny out of this shit.

I wedge me back under the window. The street lamp's givin off just enough light to read by, and I open the first book.

The writing's all funny, like a fuckin six year old. Sort of big and round and a bit wonky. Bit like Kenny. Starts after I went round his and his dad went mental.

Seventeenth of October Nineteen Seventy Five
My frend John come to tea. We had jam sandwiches, biskits,
crisps and Lemonade. Dad hurt Mum and I had four brown biskits
and five Custard Creams and he threw jam sandwiches at the wall
and he spat in my face. When I picked up the jam sandwiches I ate
some under the table when he was not looking. Mum cried all night
and so did Dad. Mum said she was sorry in the morning but I said
it did not matter. She said she is going to buy a nice present for
Christmas for me and she kissed me lots. Mum is always saying
sorry and Dad is always shouting and braking things and then he is
nice. Mum said being eleven would be better but eleven does not do
anything.

Blimey. Poor bastard. Never even realised it was his birthday. I
start skimmin. There's mad pictures what he's done everywhere, but
a fair bit of writin an all. Next bit catches me eye is when he was in
the Christmas play thing.

Seventeenth of December Nineteen Seventy Five
I looked for Mum. She was not there.

I only know it's the Christmas play thing cos he's got pictures of
stars and sheep and donkeys and the baby Jesus in a box.
Christmas comes straight after.

Twenty Fourth of December Nineteen Seventy Five
Mum said father christmas cannot get me presents but she said
we wood go for a walk in the morning TOGETHER. She said we
can go to the RIVER and see the LIGHTS on the other side. It is
raining outside my window. It looks pretty in the light like FAIRY
DUST and nothing looks REAL.

Dunno what's goin on with all them capitals. I know he's thick
and all that, but that definitely ain't right. I go to the next book and
find the bit where he first moves in with us.

Seventh of January Nineteen Seventy Six
Mrs Sissons is nice and Mr Sissons is not like dad and the little
girl is funny and if there is a GOD I want him to stop hitting my
mum. I miss my window. I want the light. My frend John is here. My

best frend John. He looks scared.

Don't be Scared John.

And there's loads of shit about his mum and dad after that, and there's loads about me, and Becky. Calls her 'the little girl'. All the way through. There was always something about Becky he really fuckin took to, like she was really special to him or something. And it's like me, Mum and Becky was everything to him. And he's got this way of writin like he's six all the way through, you know, no long words or nothing. Just simple. The bits before he got took out of school are fuckin heart-breakin. Should've see it comin. Should've been there for him.

Near the end, before he gets took away, gets to there's no dates or nothing. And the writin's all over the fuckin place.

My head is blood and black and dark and I want to cry and nobody talks to me and nobody holds my hand and I want to cry and there are no reds and blues and yellows and greens and everything is sharp and there are no edges and I want to cry.

And then a bit later on -

The little girl is yellow and her eyes shine like rainbows and I am floating and I am drowning and I am crying.

Fuck.
Poor bastard.
There's a great big gap after when Kenny got took away, then I hear this thuddin comin up the stairs. Fuckin hell, there's me gettin all sentimental when I got a fuckin job to do. And Kenny's comin up the stairs and I dunno what he'd fuckin do if he comes in here and finds me readin his little fuckin books. I start flickin through the last one. The dates are back and the writing's all back normal again. Even puts the days in. When I say 'normal', it's still like a fuckin six year old, but normal for Kenny, I mean. And there's something catches me eye what makes the whole fuckin thing make sense all at once. It's the first one after he come back here to his mum's, about a year ago.

Tuesday Sixth of September Nineteen Eighty Eight
Mr Wilkins is nice. He said if I know him from skool and I said

no. I don't know skool. I know my frend John and the little girl and Mrs Sissons and the chocolate egg and the baby Jesus but I don't know skool. He said mum died in the water and it made me sad when he said mum died in the water and he will help me go home. Mr Wilkins said to help him and he said he was my frend. He said if I know a man called Ronnie Sawfish. I said no and I said if he was a cartoon. Mr Wilkins said Mr Sawfish was not a cartoon.

***

Mr Wilkins. Fuck. Terry fuckin Wilkins. That wanker's been workin Kenny all this time, usin him to fleece Swordfish and all the while knowin when it comes, it's Kenny who's up for the chop. And if Kenny's cut what Terry's givin him is sortin Mum out with change to fuckin spare, and every other fucker round here, Terry must be gettin away with a fuckin fortune. Course, Terry knows when I come out I'm gonna suss his little game and he knows I ain't gonna just stand there and watch Kenny have it. So he's come up with this plan to wipe us both. After Kenny, he'll just get some other fuckwit to do his dirties. Ain't no way Ronnie's takin my word over Terry's, and that bastard fuckin knows it.

He's got me and Kenny by the short and fuckin curlies, and not even Ronnie Swordfish knows what's goin on.

I got that empty feelin comin over me, that feelin I got when dad passed, and when that judge sent me and Keith and Thommo down.

That feelin you get when you know there ain't a drop of hope left in the whole fuckin world.

CHAPTER TWENTY-SIX

Next day, I'm out with Charlie in the van, stockin up. Keepin busy quiets me mind, but I'm feelin cut up and sick inside. We unload at Charlie's lock-up then drive down to Elsie's on the Bethnal Green Road for a bit of breakfast.

'You all right, John?' Charlie says, chewin into his bacon sarnie.

I'm pushin a sausage round me plate like when I was a kid and didn't want me dinner, hopin if I pushed it round long enough, it'd disappear or something.

In the end, I put me knife and fork down as a lost cause.

'It's Kenny,' I says. 'He's in trouble.'

Charlie wipes his mouth with the back of his hand and puts what's left of his sarnie back on his plate. And I tell him all about Ronnie Swordfish and the money.

Charlie's hard, hard as they come. Even the likes of Brooksy would think twice about havin a tear-up with him. I tell him how I gotta get Kenny down to Wapping cos Ronnie wants a chat.

Charlie says he's comin with me, and he'll bring a few lads with him.

But this is my fight. Just like all them years ago, it was Kenny's.

'Can't do it, Charlie,' I says.

And I tell him about Mum and Becky and what Ronnie Swordfish said he'd do if I fucked with him. Charlie blows out his cheeks and scratches the back of his head, and he don't say a word. But he's fuckin ragin, I can see that. And I know he ain't keepin out of this whether I like it or not.

He asks me who else knows about it, and I tell him no one. I tell him Becky knows something's up, cos she was there when I see Terry the other day.

'Terry Wilkins?' he says.

I nod me head, and the look on Charlie's face, all red and that, tells me he'd be more than happy to chop Terry up into little bits and feed him to the ducks at the drop of a fuckin hat. He blows his cheeks out again.

He tells me Mum's up to her neck with Ronnie Swordfish, and that what Kenny's givin her's only thing keepin her head out the water.

But what Kenny's givin Mum's nicked off Ronnie Swordfish, and Charlie and Mum don't know about that. They don't even know Kenny's even workin for Ronnie, let alone nickin off him.

Don't wanna tell Charlie, though, cos then Charlie'll be on Kenny's back for gettin Mum mixed up in it all, and Kenny's in enough shit as it is.

Charlie says he was with Dad first time he went to see Swordfish. Says it was only a couple hundred, just enough to tide him and Mum over.

But that must've been ten fuckin years ago, when I were still a kid. Charlie's see the way I'm lookin, confused as fuck, and carries on.

'And there was more,' he says. And here it comes. 'When you got sent down, John,' he says, 'your Mum, she was in a right state.' His eyes narrow and the red comes in his face again.

I bend me head and me eyes get all blurred lookin at me plate. Says when she got back from the court, Terry Wilkins was waitin on her doorstep. Charlie said he tried to tell her not to, but said Wilkins was an insistent little fuck.

I can guess the rest. Terry tells Mum if there's anything him and Ronnie can do, just say the word. So Mum's gone and borrowed a load of dough to keep the fuckin wolves from the door. And, bless her, got a wedge on top just to give her and Becky some sort of fuckin life. And I know it's all my doin, the mess she's in. All my fuckin doin.

After a while, Charlie says, 'Come on, son,' and stuffs the rest of his sarnie in his mouth.

***

When I gets back, it's Becky what opens the door.

'Where's Mum?' I says.

Becky looks worried, cos she sees straight away how fuckin worried I am.

Asks me what's goin on.

'What do you mean?' I says.

Becky says she saw Kenny earlier on her way out, saw him comin out of his house with some big bag over his shoulder like he's leaving home. She says she asked him if he was all right, but he just sort of looked straight through her and carried on walking.

Shit. Kenny's done a fuckin runner, the stupid bastard.

'And Mum's never this late,' she says.

Fuck.

Next breath, there's a key in the door and Mum's come in carryin loads of shoppin, lookin proper tired.

'Sorry I'm late, dears,' she says, 'had to pick up a few bits.'

I can feel Becky's eyes burnin into me from behind cos she knows I ain't tellin her the truth.

'So, who's going to help me with this lot, then?' Mum says, smilin big.

I take the bags off her and go in the kitchen.

Becky says she'll stick the kettle on, which ain't like her, but I know it's just so she can follow me in and have a word.

And, fuck me, it is.

'I don't know what you're up to, John,' she snarls, soon as we're in the kitchen, 'but you better not be getting mixed up with that Terry Wilkins or getting Kenny into anything. Kenny's not like you or me,' she says. 'He's . . . different.'

And don't I fuckin know it.

I tell her to fuck off and leave me alone,

I really ain't got time for this shit. Mum comes in, just as Becky's about to kick off.

'Fish fingers all right, you two?' Mum says.

I don't say nothing, and Becky gets the cups out the cupboard so Mum don't see how fuckin angry she is. I tell Mum I've already ate at Elsie's, and she shakes her head, tells me all that fried food will be the death of me. If only she fuckin knew.

Becky says she ain't hungry. And now Mum knows something's up.

I finish puttin the shoppin away and go in the front room. Stick the telly on. Six o'clock news. Fuckin hate the news. Fuckin pointless. I'm about to turn it off when on comes this picture of this little Chinky geezer frontin up a tank. Frontin up a fuckin tank, I ask   you.

He's only little, this bloke, skinny as fuck. And he's carryin a couple of shoppin bags, one in each hand, like he's just come out of Tesco's or something. This tank's tryin to get past him, but he's just standin there. Won't let it come forward a fuckin inch. I sit forward in me chair. It's tryin to go past him again, movin left and right, but this cunt, he's goin with it, holdin his arms out. Gotta be fuckin mental, obviously, this geezer, but fuck me, I ain't see nothing so fuckin brave in all me fuckin life.

There's another tank comes up now, sittin behind the other, and then another one. And these are proper fuckin tanks an all. Could blow up half a fuckin street in one hit. But he don't care, this geezer. He ain't even thinkin about that. Dunno what the fuck he's thinkin about, but he ain't thinkin about that.

The geezer's climbin up on the first tank now, right up on it. Shouts down into the tank, says his piece, like, and gets back down. And that's the end of the film. End of him, I reckon an all, when they get their fuckin hands on him.

And I'm tinglin all over, sort of got this electric goin through me. Like what I had when Dad said how we was gonna beat the Arsenal, even though I knowed, and everyone else fuckin knowed, we had no fuckin chance. But it ain't always like that, see. Leastways, it weren't then. And who says it can't happen again?

And in me head I got Paul Allen through on goal, and he's chopped down by that Scotch cunt. And Paul Allen, he didn't roll round on the floor feelin sorry for himself, did he? He fuckin got straight back up like a fuckin man. And what with Paul Allen in me head and seein this little Chinky geezer and his shoppin bags frontin up these tanks, I know I can't let Kenny down. Not now.

Not again.

And that girl, George Johnson's little girl. She was only five fuckin years old. And her name was Lilly. And she needs fuckin payin for.

***

Boozer's more crowded than normal, specially for a Monday night. I clock Ronnie's geezers straight off. Two fuckin weasels, back end of the bar. Ain't seen em before, but they know who I am cos I see em joggin each other when I come in. Reckon Ronnie's holdin back his knuckle-draggers case there's any grief later.

There's a group of blokes by the bar, hard lookin. They ain't from round here. Shit. You can cut the atmosphere in here with a fuckin knife.

Charlie's talkin to Tony at the bar, and Tony waves at me to come over. Tony's ex-para. Ain't afraid of a fuckin tear-up. Can't be, runnin a boozer on this manor. I give him a nod, but I wanna be on me own for a while. Something about this whole thing ain't sittin right with me, and I only got a couple hours to figure it out.

It's Terry, see. That's what's eatin me. Ever since I known him, he ain't never been nothing other than a brown-nosin little cunt. At school, only ever picked on the littler kids and always hung about with the likes of Charlie Hamilton and Graham Allerton – the hard cunts from the year above. And in the nick he was so far up the screws' arses you couldn't find him half the fuckin time. And now he's toadyin round with Ronnie fuckin Swordfish. Terry ain't got the bottle and he ain't got the fuckin nouse to turn someone like Ronnie over from the inside. Just don't make no fuckin sense.

Besides, he's too fuckin loose with his mouth to get away with it, and trustin someone like Kenny not to fuck it up, well that's just askin for fuckin trouble, that is.

Tony calls me over. Time for business. I pull a stool up next to Charlie. I reckon Charlie must've filled Tony in with what I told him, but that ain't much, thinkin about it. Just that me and Kenny's in the shit with Ronnie Swordfish. And there's some money missin. That's it in a fuckin nutshell, when it comes down to it. Tony leans in.

'Them two over there,' he says, noddin over at Ronnie's two weasels, 'you see em before, Johnny?'

Now if those fuckers sittin there lookin over at us got any fuckin sense, they're gonna have it away on their toes quick as they fuckin can. See, every Governor on this manor's tooled up. Gotta be. And Tony ain't no different.

Someone's just spat on the back of me neck.

'Hello, shun?'

Dribblin Albert. Fuck. There's my chance wankered of makin any fuckin headway with this mess. Tony steps in.

'Here's a pint, Albert,' he says, pumpin out a freebie. 'Now fuck off, there's a good lad.'

And he does.

'That's em,' I says to Tony, gettin back to business.

'All right,' he says, and reaches under the bar. Comes out with a cricket bat and gives it to Charlie.

Charlie sticks it in his jacket and goes over to the table where Ronnie's two weasels are sittin. I can see their eyes bulgin out as he's talkin to em, and all three of em go in the toilets. Don't take a fuckin genius to know only one of em's gonna be walkin out this side of closin time.

Behind me, the door opens, and the cold blows in. So does Becky and her Gothed up mates. She ain't old enough to drink, but Tony lets her and her mates sit about, you know, cos of me dad. Becky gives me her hard look. The sort of look that'd rip your heart out if you let it. One of her mates gives her a nudge they got a seat, and Becky follows her over, still lookin straight at me. Don't want Becky round none of this. Not my little Becks. So I goes over and has a word.

Door blows in again. Kenny. Comes right up to the bar. Tony lands a coke in front of him. Same time, the phone rings and Tony hands it to Kenny. Can't see his face, but Tony can, and there's something about it that Tony knows ain't right. Not that Kenny ever give nothing away, but if you knowed him, if you really knowed him, there was little movements, you know, when he got stressed. Tiny. Round his eyes.

Kenny puts the phone down, and finishes his coke. Then he picks the phone up again, and takes a bit of paper out his pocket. Must be numbers on it, cos he's lookin at the paper and dialin what he sees. Tony's made himself scarce, servin another punter. Kenny's on the phone for just a couple of seconds then puts it down, and starts walkin.

Here he comes.

Shit. Ain't seen that face on him since the canteen.

Walks straight past me and out the door. I give it a minute, then follow him out.

And there's this motor, engine runnin, some big gorilla bastard dressed all in black holdin the door open. I'm lookin at him and he's lookin at me, and we both know I'm gettin in this motor whether I like it or not. And in the back seat, there's Kenny, lookin straight ahead.

That's when I realise, for the first time, Ronnie's callin the both of us in.

CHAPTER TWENTY-SEVEN

I'm lookin at Kenny sittin here in his shitty tracksuit bottoms and his old green anorak ripped at the arms, and he don't look like a geezer on a monkey a week. Don't look no different from when I knocked into him goin down the bins at Petticoat Lane, if I'm honest. And as for his gaff, last time that had anything done to it was when the Council cleared it out when his old girl threw herself in the River.

We ain't doin no side streets this time. Ronnie's wantin us down his place quick as a fuckin flash. Vallance Road, Whitechapel Road, headin for the A13 without so much as a fuckin red light. Kenny ain't moved a muscle since we started off. Just sittin there, he is, hands on his lap, starin at something only he can see.

'Kenny?' I says, quiet as I can, but I'm shit scared and I know it's comin out more than a whisper. 'Kenny, you all right?'

Nothing. Fuck all.

Bastard drivin turns his head round.

'Wastin your time there, mate,' he says. Tells me he had an uncle like Kenny. Tells me 'his sort' is all the fuckin same. Says they've got no brain, no better than a fuckin cabbage.

Then he laughs loud and long like it makes him feel better just to do it.

But Kenny ain't like that. He ain't like what he says. Just no one sees it. Keeps it all hid. Safe, you know. And it's like he's got it sorted more than all the rest of us put together, like he's on the inside and it's the rest of us on the outside's tryin to get in, tryin to understand. And we can't do it, cos we're too fuckin busy runnin.

Car's bumpin over all sorts of shit, and the fog's comin down off the River. Wasteland. Fuck.

'Here we are, boys. Time to move.'

But Kenny ain't goin nowhere.

'Kenny?' I says. 'Come on, mate. We gotta see Ronnie.'

I see his chest goin up and down. Heavin. Real deep. He's breathin through his nose and his mouth's tight shut, just like you do when you're about to do something really fuckin scary.

The fuckin idiot what drove us down here tells us to leave our coats in the motor.

Wants to know we ain't got no fuckin shooters or blades or nothing. Fair enough, really. I chuck me coat on the back seat. Kenny takes off his anorak and lays it careful on the back seat with mine. And he's wearin the whitest shirt I ever fuckin see. Got all the buttons an all. Can't help smilin, even though I'm fuckin cackin myself.

What with his shitty tracksuit bottoms and this white shirt, and his brown shoes what I just noticed, I reckon he must be keepin every fuckin charity shop this side of the River in business all his fuckin self.

Something's clickin in me, lookin at him, like the wheels are turnin and it's all openin up. It's fuckin right in front of me. Kenny. If Kenny's thievin off Ronnie Swordfish, what the fuck's he doin lookin like a catalogue model out of fuckin Oxfam? If he had the brains to be skimmin the cream off Ronnie, he'd least smarten himself up a bit, fuckin surely.

We're slippin over bricks and mud, headin towards Ronnie's gaff, and Kenny don't even break his stride. It's like when I was a kid and thinkin he could walk through a fuckin brick wall when he was like this.

It's fuckin freezin, what with the fog, and the River bein so close, and me jaw's shakin. Not to mention bein more scared than I been me whole fuckin life. I'm gettin the feelin I fucked up along the way, and I'm about to find out how. Been thinkin so hard about Kenny, bleedin forgot my part in all this fuckin shambles.

Ronnie's gaff's comin up out the fog. Brooksy's standin outside, and the door's openin. Ronnie's out first, then Terry behind him, and four others. I'm guessin the others are the same ones what was sittin round the table first time I was here. The inner fuckin circle. Ronnie comes forward, sort of stridin. Ain't hard to tell he's one angry cunt.

I reckon I can outrun em all. But Kenny, he's too big a lump, so that's a non-fuckin-starter. And a bullet in the back's no way to fuckin go. Just gettin desperate, that's all. I'm lookin about me, left and right, dunno what I'm lookin for cos there ain't no fuckin way out of this now. I look across at Kenny.

And Kenny's walkin through mountains.

Ronnie's stopped, and he's standin there, waitin. The others are lined up behind him, like a barbed wire fence. There's about six foot between us and them.

And Ronnie don't stand on no fuckin ceremony. Gets straight in there.

'Where's my fucking money?'

He's gone right up close to Kenny now, nose to fuckin nose. Funny thing is, Ronnie's about six inches shorter than Kenny, so he's sort of lookin upward as he does it. Can't help smilin a bit, but only cos I'm fuckin terrified.

Kenny don't say a word. I'm lookin at Terry now, cos if Terry's usin Kenny to fleece Ronnie, like I reckon, it'd be writ all over his fuckin face. But there ain't a fuckin glimmer. And that does it for me. That fuckin does it.

And I wanna tell Ronnie, but Ronnie's too busy shoutin his mouth off.

I wanna tell him Kenny ain't nickin nothing. Just he's givin all what Ronnie's payin him to Mum and what Mum gives back to him, he's givin out to whatever other poor fuckers need it. I mean, come on, what's the likes of Kenny gonna do with two grand a month? All he's after's enough to keep himself fed and watered and some spendin money down the charities. Probably dosses at his mum's when the weather's shit, and the rest of the times he's livin on the streets and goin down the bins like he always done. Ronnie, he's heard Kenny's been flashin his cash and the suspicious fuck's assumed he must be on the take.

Thing is, Kenny's little Robin Hood act's fuckin up Ronnie's loan-sharkin business big time, so no way Ronnie's fuckin standin by and lettin that happen.

Kenny still ain't sayin nothing. Fuck, he ain't even moved. Leastways, not that no one else can see. But I do. Something's changin in him. That glue in his eyes what's always been there, it's fallin. Fallin away. And there's burnin behind it.

I gotta say something. Gotta stop it. Buy a bit of fuckin time at least.

'Ronnie?' I says. 'Ronnie?'

He turns his head to me, and his face is red and shiny and his eyes are so big, looks like they're gonna fuckin burst right out.

'And you,' he shouts, meanin me, 'I ain't even fucking started on you yet, you cunt, so do yourself a fucking favour and keep your fucking mouth shut. All right?'

Brooksy's come forward to stand next to Ronnie, facin me. I know I fucked up the minute I knocked down Kenny's front door. Ronnie musta knowed I'd try and tip Kenny off to find a way out. I was so fucked up with it all, never even thought to keep a look out for any of Ronnie's monkeys.

Brooksy's lookin at me like he wants to fuckin eat me. He's got a metal bar in his hand. Weapon of choice for your proper fuckin psycho, that is. And he ain't wackin his other palm with it like you see in the films. He's just holdin it, like you would a fuckin bread roll or a rolled up fuckin newspaper.

Ronnie's on the way to proper fuckin losin it now. He's pushin Kenny, but Kenny don't move a fuckin inch. Stands there like a tree what's been growin there a thousand years.

And the glue's still fallin.

Brooksy's see something. He's lookin past me. Behind me. And his knuckles have gone white round the metal bar where he's holdin it tighter. I daren't fuckin turn round case he fuckin lumps me one, but something's occurring.

He's tryin to say something to Ronnie, but Ronnie don't hear. Ronnie's in a place all his fuckin own, and he tells Terry Wilkins to fetch his sword.

Fuck. This is it.

Terry can't think of nothing else he'd rather fuckin do and he's in and out the cabin like Linford fuckin Christie.

Now's me only chance.

'Ronnie?' I says, 'It ain't Kenny, Kenny ain't takin nothing, he –.'

But Ronnie ain't listenin.

'Shut that cunt up, Brooksy,' he says, meanin me again.

And Brooksy, like he's on automatic fuckin pilot, cracks me round the side of the head with the metal bar.

Everything goes quiet. I can feel meself fallin, but it's like in slow motion, and I can see this big fuckin grin on Brooksy's face like the whole world suddenly makes sense to him again. And I know I'm on the ground but I don't feel the ground, and it's like I'm floatin. And everything's quiet. Brooksy's tryin to say something to Ronnie, and he's pointin behind me, and Terry's comin up with the sword.

I'm lookin at the sky and I'm lookin at the stars and I'm thinkin the moon's like this great big ball of light, just like the one outside Kenny's window. And lookin at it, I'm gettin closer to Kenny, closer to what it's like bein him all these years.

I turn me head. Neither Ronnie or Brooksy see me cos they think I'm fuckin out of it. And behind me, all lit up by the moon, what Brooksy's lookin at is people, standin on piles of brick and dirt and pallets. Loads of em. I squint me eyes a bit so I can see proper. And there's all the locals from the pub, blokes what knowed Dad all his life, and there's blokes from the football, and the factory. Don't even know half their names. But I recognise em all. And there's the hard blokes that was in the boozer, Charlie's mates, I reckon, and there's women an all. And everyone's tooled up. Half cut bricks, broken bottles, fuckin anything they can fuckin get. And right up front there's Charlie and Tony, and next to them, right at the sharp end, Becky, standin brave as the rest.

They know they can't do nothing cos, I mean Kenny's got a fuckin sword to his head, but just them bein there means the fuckin world.

I turn back to Ronnie, and I'm smilin up at him, not that he can see me, of course. He's got the sword in his hand now, and seein that soon wipes the smile off me face. Slow motion, he's liftin the fuckin thing over his head. Then he stops, and his face goes all fuckin grey. Something else has gone off. Terry's doin a runner out past the back of the Portacabin and Brooksy, he's scarperin, and all the others, they're all havin it away on their toes.

Then me ears pop from where I got hammered, and me hearin comes back.

Sirens. Police sirens. Fuckin hundreds of em.

Ronnie's lookin at Kenny. Lookin right in his face. Hard, like he's tryin to work something out. And Kenny's lookin right back at him. Then Ronnie, with his other hand, pulls open Kenny's shirt. And, fuck me, Kenny's wired up like the national fuckin grid.

The words of Kenny's diary hit me right in the face, harder than Brooksy's metal pole.

Mr Wilkins said to help him.

Old Bill's swarmin all over the gaff, and I'm tryin to get so I can take Swordfish down cos he's lifted that sword up again, but I can't move me legs. Then I see the look in Kenny's eyes. There ain't no glue no more. And his eyes are big and soft and shinin and meltin all at the same time. And Ronnie's seen it and he don't know what to do. He's hesitatin. With everything I got, I go for his legs.

I'd die for Kenny right now. I'd die for his courage and his kindness and his grubby tracksuit bottoms and his brown fuckin shoes. And for that look in his eyes, I'd die a thousand fuckin times. But me legs is gone, and Ronnie's face is all squeezed tight and he's roarin like a fuckin animal. He brings his sword down like he's tryin to chop the whole world in half. There's an Old Bill gets there just too late, takes Swordfish down and he's fightin with him in the dirt. When he gets up, his helmet's off and he's got Ronnie in handcuffs. And who'd have thought it? Harry fuckin Wilkins. No wonder Terry didn't wanna talk about him.

Harry's draggin Ronnie away backwards. Ronnie's still roarin, and Harry's got tears runnin through the dirt on his face and he can't take his eyes off Kenny lyin in the mud.

***

Turns out Harry Wilkins weren't a bad sort. Said some nice stuff at Kenny's funeral, all in his uniform and everything. Went right back to school, he did. Didn't leave nothing out.

Really fucked him up when Kenny sorted him out in the canteen all them years back. Even went to visit him in the nut-house. When Harry saw Kenny goin down the bins when he got out, he felt right bad, thinkin it was him that done it to the poor bastard. Wanted to make it up and thought he could get even with Terry at the same time. See, Terry'd beat the shit out of Harry from the day he was born. All body stuff, you know, like the old man taught him. No wonder the poor fucker got like he did with Kenny. Had to take it out somewhere.

Harry sorted Kenny out with the house and his mum's funeral, and stuff. Was really good to him, you know. His Governor was after Swordfish, but it was Terry what Harry was after. In the end, what with Kenny's diaries and all the other monkeys on the Firm grassin each other up left, right and fuckin centre, not a one of em got away with less than a fifteen stretch. And Swordfish, he won't see the light of day the rest of his fuckin life.

They buried Kenny with his mum in Barking Cemetery. Place was packed. People said they never see nothing like it.

***

It's been a year since Kenny's gone. I think about him every day.

I see him sometimes. In me dreams, or if I close me eyes real tight. And he's lookin at me. Just lookin. And his eyes, they're big and they're bright and they're shinin, and it's like he talks to me with em. And when I squeeze me eyes even tighter and look really close, his eyes shine even more. And they're just like what he said about Becky's all them years back in his diary.

And that's when it really gets me, that's what makes me really fuckin sad. Cos behind that glue, underneath all that shit what ended up bein his life, those eyes of his, they never stopped shinin.

Shinin like fuckin rainbows.

THE END